# The Rose
# and the Duke

*Ravishing Rosewoods, Book 1*

By Jillian Eaton

This is a work of fiction. Names, characters, places and incidents are either the product of the author's imagination or are used fictitiously, and any resemblance to actual persons, living or dead, business establishments, events, or locales is entirely coincidental.

Cover: Dar Albert, Wicked Smart Designs

ISBN: 9798421931591

Printed in the U.S.A.

*Four roses, pretty and fair*
*All with different color hair*
*Lenora, stern and strict and wise*
*Bridget, quiet, bookish, and shy*
*Annabel who wants happily after*
*Eloise who will bend to no master*
*In their secret garden waiting*
*For a man to set their heart racing...*

# DEDICATION

*For my dear husband.*

*Who didn't flinch on our 3rd date when I said,*

*"I think I want to quit my job and be an author".*

# PROLOGUE

### *A Rogue in the Hand is Worth Two in the Parlor*

Clarenmore Park

Mid-Summer 1869

"I COULD TAKE YOU RIGHT here, if I so desired." Perth spoke so brusquely, so casually, that the meaning of his words did not register for Lenora at first.

When they did, when she followed his hot, carnal stare to the settee against the windowsill, her breath caught and heat filled her belly, going all the way up into her cheeks. Blushing, she turned away from him to stare blindly at a painting on the wall. Outside the parlor there came the dim sound of voices and the clinking of porcelain. The other house guests, milling about the foyer as they enjoyed a picnic luncheon that had spilled in from outside. Inside the parlor it was quiet, save for the quiet rasp of her breath and the pounding of her heart.

"You–you shouldn't say such things," she murmured.

"Why not?" His boots sank silently into the thick Aubusson rug as he prowled up behind her, carrying with him the scent of sandalwood and a hint of leather. It was a rugged, masculine scent. But then Perth was a rugged, masculine man. All raw strength and charming wit and sly innuendos.

She gasped out loud when his fingers traced the delicate vertebrae in her neck. He wasn't wearing gloves, and the bare touch of his flesh to hers was shockingly sensual. She felt the warm fan of his breath across her skin and her throat went dry when he nudged her hair to the side and kissed her nape.

"This is not proper, Your Grace." Her hands knotted into fists, nails digging into her palms through satin fabric.

"No," he agreed. "Probably not. But you don't want to be proper all the time, do you Lenora? That's all right." He used his teeth to loosen the ribbon tie at the top of her gown while simultaneously grasping her hips and pulling her snug against him. "I won't reveal to anyone that prim, perfect Lady Lenora has a naughty streak. Should I tell you what I want to do to you?"

*No.*

*No, no, no.*

"Yes," she whimpered.

*Oh, yes.*

His hands rose slowly up her body, following its natural curves before sliding around to cup her breasts. He flicked his thumbs across her nipples, coaxing them into hard little buds that strained against the confines of her bodice.

"First I'd memorize every inch of you," he said huskily. "Every peak and valley. From that plump mouth begging to be kissed to the curls between your thighs. Tell me, Lenora." His tongue traced the outside shell of her ear as his voice continued to wash over her in a long, searing wave of wickedness. "Have you ever touched yourself down there? At midnight with the moon high and your body restless, have you stroked between those soft curls to the pearl underneath?"

Her cheeks burned. "N-no."

"*Liar*," he whispered as his fingers forged an inquisitive path across her ribcage. "Were you wet, Lenora? Are you wet now?"

Her knees wobbled when he gently rubbed her through her skirts. She *was* wet. But she dared not make such a sinful admission. Not to him. Not to this man who infuriated her as much as he aroused her.

Electrical currents pulsed through her body, centered right beneath the hand that stroked and massaged and coaxed forth even more slippery dampness. Another whimper wrenched free of her lips when he bit her earlobe, drawing the sensitive flesh into his mouth to lick in tandem with the lazy undulation of his wrist.

Who was this woman, she wondered dazedly? This woman who would lean wantonly against a duke, allowing him to pleasure her at his will while her houseguests milled right outside the unlocked door?

She was a step from ruin...and for once, she didn't care.

Such was Perth's power over her.

His influence.

She was caught in his thrall, and in that moment, in that precise *second*, there was nowhere else she'd rather be but wrapped in his arms.

No matter that he was a rogue.

No matter that she despised him.

No matter that there was no future between them.

"I could bring you to release right here, standing on your feet in the middle of the room where you had tea this morning." Perth hadn't shaved yet today, and rough stubble on his jaw against her smooth skin made her toes curl as he nuzzled the tiny space where her neck and shoulder joined. "Would you like that, Lenora? Would you like to come for me...again?"

Heaven help her, but she would.

Her chin betrayed her as it bobbed up and down; the smallest of acquiesces.

A possessive growl rumbled low in the depths of Perth's throat. Keeping his hand in the middle of her thighs, he spun her around to face him, the violent action tempered by unexpected gentleness as he cupped her face, his large hand effortlessly spanning across her flushed cheek to the tendrils of hair that had escaped from her coiffure.

"Aye, you'd love it." His eyes, dark and savage, gleamed into hers. Gone was the charismatic, devil-may-care duke. He'd been replaced by a far more dangerous version of Perth. A hard, demanding rogue who took what he wanted, when he wanted it…and what he wanted was her. "I'd back you up against the wall. Pin your arms above your head as I ripped your gown away. Buttons and thread. Lace and muslin. It would pool at your feet as I took your breast into my mouth. Would you like that? If I kissed you there. And here." His fingers pulsated between her legs.

Trembling, she nodded again.

And then the door opened.

# 1

## *Sisters Can be Most Egregious*

Clarenmore Park
Sixteen Days Ago

"ELOISE, IF YOU DO NOT come down from that tree this instant, I am going to scream!" Coming from Lenora Rosewood, it was a grave threat indeed.

Lenora never raised her voice. Or spoke out of turn. Or said anything that might be deemed inappropriate or unwise. She was an impeccable example of what a lady of fine breeding and excellent manners should act like.

Her sister, Eloise, on the other hand, was...

Not.

There were five of them in all. Four sisters and a

brother, James, the Earl of Clarenmore, who'd left eleven months ago on his Grand Tour and never returned.

He *was* going to come back.

Someday.

But until he did, that left Lenora, as the next eldest, in charge of her siblings.

There was Bridget, sweet and shy, who had her nose buried in a book more often than not. Annabel, whose natural beauty and charm was renowned throughout the *ton*. And then there was Eloise, who was currently hiding in a tree in a ridiculous attempt to avoid her much-loathed weekly embroidery lesson.

"I can see your foot," Lenora said between gritted teeth. "And if *I* can see your foot that means *other* people can see your foot, and no one should see your foot, Eloise. Least of all without a stocking on it!"

"There's no one else here but you," came Eloise's defiant reply from somewhere amidst the green canopy of oak leaves.

"We've a household full of servants," Lenora countered as she clung to the vestiges of her rapidly waning patience. "Not to mention the two dozen guests who will be descending upon us later this afternoon. Or have you forgotten about the house party?"

An indelicate snort, and then…

"Why do you think I'm hiding in this bloody tree?"

"*Eloise!*"

Bare feet in trees was one thing, but use of such

language was quite another. Although to be fair, the youngest and most belligerent Rosewood sister came by it honestly.

Their father, a gruff, stately man whose brown eyes had twinkled whenever he'd beheld his daughters, had possessed the bad habit of bringing curses home with him from the horse races he had loved to frequent.

When she was a child, Lenora used to find it highly amusing when the earl, predisposed to a stern nature, had sworn like a common sailor over a stubbed toe or a spilled cup of tea. Now, as an adult responsible for the wellbeing and security of her family, she understood why her mother's eyes had rolled towards the heavens with every blast, bloody, and damn.

"I don't want people to come here." Eloise swung her leg in open rebellion. "I don't want a house party."

Neither did Lenora, but then there were a *lot* of things that she didn't want. And a lot of things that she did. But if the past year and a half had taught her anything, it was that wanting–or the lack of it–did not bring things to pass.

Steely determination, desperate faith, and blind luck did.

"Should I send Bridget out?" she asked pointedly.

It was her last ploy. Short of climbing up into the damned tree herself (Lenora was capable of swearing too, but only in her head) and forcibly removing Eloise from the branch she was perched on like some sort of flightless bird, she had nothing else. Nothing but to threaten one sister with another. And none of them–not herself, not Annabel, and not even Eloise–could deny Bridget anything.

"If she's inside reading, don't bother her. She's just got her hands on a new book from that author she is in love with. Although how she reads all that French without her eyes crossing is a mystery to me." A long pause, followed by a dramatic sigh. "I'll come down, I *suppose.*"

There was a loud rustle of leaves, another curse, and then Eloise dropped to the ground at Lenora's feet in a pile of blue linen, tangled red hair, and surly defiance.

Extending her hand, Lenora pulled her sister upright.

"You are fortunate that you didn't injure yourself," she scolded gently as they made their way back to the manor. "You're too old to be hiding in trees."

At eighteen, Eloise was five years Lenora's junior. After the birth of her firstborn son, Lady Catherine Rosewood suffered a miscarriage before she welcomed four daughters. Lenora, Bridget, Annabel, and Eloise. Unfortunately, her health had declined with each subsequent pregnancy. She'd wanted even more children. A baby for each bedroom, she used to say, and Clarenmore Park boasted twenty-two bedchambers in total. But her doctor had advised against it, and thus Eloise became the last Rosewood to be born...and was spoiled endlessly as a result, which had surely contributed to her rebellious spirit. That, and by the time she came of age to learn rules and manners, their nannies were so overwhelmed that she was largely left to her own devices.

Since the death of their parents, James was the one family member that she remotely listened to. And now with *him* gone, managing Eloise had turned into a full-time job for Lenora. In addition to looking after Bridget, Annabel, Clarenmore Park, the servants, and the stables that held what remained of her father's precious breeding stock. Not to mention managing the townhouse in Grosvenor Square, planning their annual summer house party, and curating a pool of suitable suitors from which her sisters could choose their future husband.

Suffice it to say, Lenora did *not* have time to be pulling Eloise out of trees. If only James was here. Eloise wouldn't be nearly as brazen in her disobedience. But their brother had wanted–and deserved–to go on a Grand Tour.

Most young men took a year or more to sow their wild oats and see the world before they settled down into their title; James had wanted six months. Six months of reckless adventuring across two continents before he came home and assumed his responsibilities as earl, a title that none of them had ever anticipated he'd inherit so soon.

The death of their parents had come as a shock to the Rosewood siblings. Lady Catherine passed during the winter. Her health, always fragile, had taken a turn for the worse following a difficult bout of pneumonia. After she passed, their father sank into a deep depression. To this day, no one knew why he'd gone walking on the lake that morning. It was well known that the ice was dangerously thin in some spots. There were even rumors that past ancestors had died trying to cross it. And on that frosty dawn in the middle of February, the freezing waters claimed another Rosewood life.

After the tragic losses, James abandoned his bachelor life that he'd been enjoying in London to return to Clarenmore Park and care for his sisters. He'd comforted them in their grief, and had held the family together as they'd adjusted to living without their mother's gentle support or their father's steady guidance. But he had soon begun to grow restless, even before their first year of mourning had reached its conclusion.

He never dared say anything. He wouldn't hurt them. Not on purpose. But Lenora could see it in his eyes. In the rigid set of his shoulders. In the way he'd gaze longingly at the horses whenever they'd go into a full gallop and vanish over the hill.

She'd always had a way of feeling the emotions of those closest to her. A talent that was as much a curse as it was a gift. That was how she'd known that James was discontent. And why she had encouraged him to leave. Because he would be a better earl, a better *brother*, if he didn't spend the rest of his life secretly yearning for what might have been…and hating himself for it all the while.

Ironically, he'd resisted at first. He hadn't wanted to leave them. Such was his devotion to family. But Lenora was insistent. After all, what was six months? With Eloise still a year shy of making her debut, she had already decided to keep her sisters in the country for one more season. When James returned, they'd all go to London together. A relaunch into High Society that would be guaranteed to attract attention, especially after such a long absence.

Annabel, blessed with stunning beauty, would have a dozen offers for her hand before the first week was out. Bridget would find a nice gentleman who enjoyed reading by the fire. And Eloise...well, Eloise would be Eloise.

It was a perfect plan. And Lenora *did* like her plans.

Rules and order and responsibility were her constant companions. They'd held her hand through her agonizing sorrow, and had helped her make sense of a world without her parents in it. Without her mother in it. Because a woman was meant to have her mother, whether she was a little girl or a lady full grown.

During the first three months of his travels, James had written them nearly every week. Long paragraphs detailing his exploits in Spain, Italy, and Greece. All harbor stops on the way to his ultimate destination: Bombay. The last letter to arrive spoke of his excitement at sailing the Suez Canal, a narrow waterway that connected the Mediterranean Sea to the Red Sea and made it possible to travel to India in less than eight weeks; a journey that used to take half a year or more. He'd wanted to see an elephant in the wild, and climb the Satpura Range, and visit an old friend who he'd not seen since his days at Oxford.

His sisters had awaited his next letter with breathless anticipation...but it never came. They'd tried sending letters of their own, which either returned to them unopened or simply disappeared. When the date of his return came and went, they hired a private investigator, but his search led to more questions than answers.

March and April yielded nothing but spring rains.

May and June brought flowers, but no brother.

Now July was here, hot and sticky.

They were hours away from the house party; the first time they'd held it since their parent's death.

And James...James was nowhere to be found.

Lenora knew that Eloise, Bridget, and Annabel feared the worst.

*She* feared the worst.

But she couldn't let on about the true state of their brother's welfare. Or lack thereof. None of them could. For all anyone else knew, he was still on his Grand Tour. Because if James was declared deceased, then that would mean their odious cousin, Mr. Richard Rosewood, would inherit the earldom and all that went with it. Including their much beloved Clarenmore Park, the manor in Grosvenor Square, their father's horses...even their dowries. What remained of them, that is.

All of it, every penny, every stick of furniture, every painting, would go to Richard.

They'd be at the mercy of a conniving, arrogant man who'd just as soon smirk at them as toss them out with only the clothes on their back. *If* he happened to be feeling generous. Otherwise, he'd insist that they leave their dresses behind as well.

Since Lenora could not allow that to happen–*would* not allow it–she'd been exceedingly careful to maintain the illusion that James was soon to come home. Any day. Any minute, really. Until he did, she would continue to look after everything in his stead. Including her sisters. A gargantuan task made all the more exceedingly difficult when one of them behaved more like a squirrel than a debutante.

"Mrs. Broderick is not the evil witch you portray her to be," she began, referring to the seamstress whom Eloise had been hiding from. "And embroidery is a skill-"

"That every gentleman expects of a docile, well-educated lady," Eloise sighed. "So you've said. But I don't *want* to be docile and surely there is more to education than stabbing a needle through a bit of cloth. What of history, science, and battlefield management?"

Lenora arched a dark brow. While Eloise, with her fiery mop of red curls and stubborn chin, took after their grandmother, long deceased, she'd inherited her ebony hair and somber, serious blue gaze from their mother.

"Battlefield management?" she repeated dubiously as they entered the main foyer and she automatically handed off her gloves and hat to a waiting footman. "What on earth would you need that for?"

Eloise, who was wearing neither gloves *nor* a hat, gave a sharp jerk of her shoulder before she flounced into the adjourning parlor and sprawled in dramatic fashion upon a velvet upholstered settee. "Men learn of such things at Oxford and Eton. Why not I?"

Discreetly closing the door behind her (while the servants were accustomed to Eloise lying about with all the dignity of a cat sunning itself on a windowsill, there was no telling when guests would start to arrive), Lenora stepped into the room and poured them both some freshly made lemonade.

"Here," she said, extending a glass towards her sister.

"Thank you." Tilting her head back, Eloise guzzled the lemonade and then smacked her lips. "Delicious."

Lenora pressed her thumb and index finger to the bridge of her nose where a dull ache was beginning to settle. "Eloise–"

"I already know what you're going to say," her sister interrupted with a roll of her eyes. "The same as you always do. I must mend my behavior and devote myself to more feminine pursuits in the hopes that I might land a titled husband with enough wealth to sustain my spending habits. Except I don't *like* feminine pursuits and I don't *want* a husband and I don't *have* a spending habit." Her lower lip jutted, much as it had when she was a child and their mother had denied her a second slice of cake. "So there."

When annoyance surged, Lenora tempered it. She did not anger easily. But if there was anyone who knew where to poke and press, it was Eloise. Still, it wouldn't do to yell or lecture. She'd all but recited *The True Ladies Manual of Politeness and Etiquette* word for word, and it had gone in one ear and right out the other. That being said, she wasn't about to allow herself to be trod over. Maintaining a sense of governance over her brood of siblings was just as important as maintaining the illusion that James was soon to return. Both offered stability. A sense of purpose. A common goal. And if either of them vanished, chaos would ensue.

If there was one thing Lenora could not abide, it was chaos.

"Actually, I was just going to tell you that you've a spider on your arm," she said innocently, and hid a grin behind her glass of lemonade when Eloise–who *hated* spiders–shrieked and leapt to her feet while simultaneously wiggling about and throwing her hands in the air as if performing some new deranged waltz.

"What on earth is going on?" Annabel demanded when she entered the parlor with her customary long limbed grace. Tendrils of chestnut hair twisted through with blonde framed a slender face that boasted perfect symmetry. Winged brows arched high above cornflower blue eyes, prominent cheekbones, and a straight nose with only the tiniest bit of a tilt at the end. All of the Rosewood sisters were attractive in their own right, but Annabel was unquestionably the prettiest. A fact that she was very well aware of, and not above using for her own means.

As she'd once told Lenora, if men could weaponize their strength, why could women not use their beauty as they might a dagger? To twist, and turn, and gain themselves the leverage that a Society designed for the comfort of their male counterparts did not give willingly.

"You said there was a spider, didn't you?" she said.

"It's an old, drafty manor. I am certain there *is* a spider. Somewhere," Lenora amended.

Annabel shook her head. "That's a wicked thing to do, Nora." She glanced at Eloise, who was still dancing about, and a dimple flashed high in her right cheek as she grinned. "But amusing. Was she hiding in a tree again?"

"The oak in the front this time," Lenora confirmed with a sigh. "Nearly took half an hour of badgering before she'd come down. What are we to do with her? She may be the youngest, but she's not a child anymore."

"Is it gone?" Eloise asked frantically as she hopped from one foot to another. "Is it gone?"

"I'd check your hair," Annabel said with a vague flourish of her arm before she turned her attention back to Lenora. "No, Eloise is not a child. But if you're so keen on marrying us off, she has a few years before the *ton* starts calling her a spinster. I'd be more concerned with Bridget."

"Bridget isn't climbing trees or wanting to learn about strategies of war."

"No, but she's rarely seen out of the library."

"Men like quiet, well-read women."

"Do they?" Annabel said with a skeptical tilt of her head.

*I hope so*, Lenora thought silently. Or else Bridget's future prospects *would* be of concern.

"What about you?" Annabel went on. "When do you plan to marry? You *are* the eldest. Shouldn't you be leading by example?"

Marriage?

Lenora's blood ran cold at the thought.

When she was a young girl with a head full of dreams and a heart filled with butterflies, it was all she'd dreamt about. Marriage to a dashing earl or a handsome viscount. A man who would recite poetry on bended knee and compliment the way the sunlight glimmered in her hair. He would be both strong and gentle, a warrior and a scholar, and they'd fall in love and marry and raise a family.

Such was her plan...until her parents died, and her brother disappeared, and Cousin Richard started circling them like a buzzard.

Marry?

She couldn't *marry*.

Not until Bridget, Annabel, and Eloise found husbands, at any rate.

That was her job now. To ensure their future prosperity and happiness, even if it came at the sake of her own. Because that was what a sister did. What their mother *would* have done, if she was still alive.

"You had the benefit of three Seasons," Annabel went on, oblivious to the sudden stiffness in Lenora's shoulders. "I'm sure you met dozens of eligible candidates. Now that we're more than a year out of mourning, you should encourage their suit with a letter. How are you, I've been thinking about you, let's get married. Something along those lines."

"That may be a tad too direct."

"You know what I mean. You can't stay at Clarenmore *forever*, Nora. It's meant to be a house, not a prison."

Lenora's lips parted. "I never said it was a–"

"There wasn't a spider on me, was there?" Marching over to them, Eloise delivered a swift and not-so-gentle punch to Lenora's arm. "You bully. You know how scared of them I am. They've far too many legs. And they're *hairy*. Have you ever looked at one up close? They have fangs." She brought two fingers to her mouth and wiggled them. "*Yeck.* That was mean, Nora. Really mean. Cruel, even."

Lenora rubbed her arm. "So was hiding in a tree to avoid your embroidery lesson. A lesson that you've now missed, mind you."

"There'll be another next week."

"Next month, you mean. All lessons and classes will be postponed until the end of the house party."

"That's *one* silver lining, I suppose."

"You enjoyed the last house party," Annabel pointed out.

"That's because I could sit at the children's table and stay up late spying on the adults and eat chocolate to my heart's content." A shadow rippled across Eloise's countenance. "And Mother and Father were still here," she finished softly.

All three sisters fell silent.

"Well," Lenora said after a long pause, because she needed to say something, *anything*, to breathe air back into the room before they all suffocated beneath the weight of their grief. "We're here. The four of us. Together. And I'm sure I have some chocolate tucked away somewhere."

After their parents died, Lenora was told by several people, all well-intentioned, that she would feel better in time. As if time was the magical healer of all hurts, and once enough of it had gone by her anguish and her sadness would just…disappear. But if there was anything that she had learned over the past two years, it was that grief wasn't a river, running in one direction until it eventually spilled into the ocean. Rather, it *was* the ocean. Ebbing and flowing. Sometimes calm and other times rolling, restless, and wild.

You didn't forget the storm. You *never* forgot the storm. Instead you learned to live with it. To adjust your sails and plunge headfirst into the hurt because that was the only way through to the healing.

"We should get ready." Annabel, never one for tears (she hated when her eyes turned red and puffy) clapped her hands briskly together. "Guests will begin arriving soon, and I know that I, for one, need to change."

Eloise cast a dubious glance at her sister's flawless hair, pearl earrings, and peach-colored gown with stripes of white silk and matching pearls painstakingly stitched along the bodice. "What's wrong with what you have on?"

"This old thing?" Annabel said, horrified. "I can't wear *this* to greet my future husband. He'll think I am one of the maids."

To Eloise's credit, she waited until Annabel had flounced out of the room to groan and say, "If that's what you want me to turn into, it's never going to happen."

"I want you to be yourself," Lenora chided. Spying a piece of green amidst all of her sister's riotous red curls, she sighed as she pulled out a leafy twig. "Maybe just not with so many sticks in your hair."

# 2

## *All You're Missing is a Skirt*

PERTH ROBERT STEWART, 8th Duke of Monmouth, despised house parties. He bloody *loathed* them. Trapped under a roof with marriage-hungry debutantes for an entire month? He'd rather cast himself over the rail into shark infested waters and take his chances swimming to shore, thank you very much. Which was why he'd done his best to avoid them like the plague, and he was rather proud of the excuses that he had managed to come up with over the years.

Illness was an obvious choice.

His carriage got lost and somehow ended up at a pub in the highlands (he hated it when that happened).

His valet mixed up the dates.

He was away on business.

He was away on holiday.

A death in the family.

Then there really *was* a death in the family. His father, the 7th Duke of Monmouth. A right bastard of a man in personality if not blood. Whom Perth had despised almost as much as he did house parties.

Still, he hadn't rejoiced in his father's untimely demise. Unlike most firstborn sons, Perth had not been chomping at the bit to inherit his title. Not when he had been getting along splendidly as a marquess, at any rate. All of the fun and none of the responsibility that came with a dukedom. For all he'd cared, his sire could have lived to a hundred.

Instead, the old goat had choked to death on a plum. An undignified end made even more darkly humorous by the fact that he had been eating said fruit in the bed of his mistress, an opera singer of dubious origins who had risen to fame courtesy of her very talented…mouth.

Neither Perth nor his mother, Anastasia, who much preferred being the Dowager Duchess of Monmouth than the duchess, had spent much time mourning the late duke's passing. He'd been miserable to them both, and while they hadn't spit on his grave, there may have been a glass or two of champagne raised in celebration of his death.

After seeing that his mother was comfortably settled and the opera singer duly compensated (no amount of money could make up for having a hairy boar die on top of her, but a thousand pounds could buy discretion), Perth set about discovering what duties awaited him as the newly minted Duke of Monmouth. Aside from lots of Your Graces, presiding over a much larger estate in Shaffordshire, and a seat with a better view in the House of Lords, he was pleased to find that it wasn't *that* much different.

With one looming exception.

The Rosewood's annual summer house party.

For reasons that escaped him, his mother was insistent–*insistent*–on attending. It appeared she and Lady Clarenmore, now deceased, had had a close friendship, and she wanted to see how the woman's daughters were getting on. Precisely what letters were for, in Perth's humble opinion. But the dowager duchess was adamant that she see the chits in person, and as her husband was no longer alive to accompany her, the duty fell to her son.

And that was how he found himself in a carriage bound for Clarenmore Park, an estate set at the end of a long, winding stone drive lined on either side with large, stately common oaks in their full summer foliage. The drive ended on a full circle in front of a sprawling stone manor with ivy creeping up the side and a row of matching turrets protruding from a gray slate roof.

It was a grand manor, albeit a tad shabby at the edges. The row of boxwoods framing the front wall needed to be cut back and the stone replenished in spots, but the windows sparkled with cleanliness and colorful flowers spilled from an eclectic collection of pots and wooden troughs scattered strategically along the front of the estate to soften its hard angles and straight, formal lines. All in all, as Perth disembarked from the carriage and turned to assist his mother, he was reminded of his Aunt Tabitha.

His father's only living relation aside from himself, Aunt Tabby's bloodlines could be traced all the way back to a distant cousin of King George—the very first George, not the mad one that lost Britain the American colonies. But for all her fine breeding, Aunt Tabby had always been a tad…rumpled. Mismatched stockings, feathers in her hair, a live weasel named Mr. Prendergast that she'd worn draped around her neck instead of a proper mink stole.

Clarenmore Park was rather like that. Good bones, but teetering on the brink of dishevelment. Making him wonder if the earl didn't have a gambling problem. If so, they were going to get on exceptionally well. Except last he'd heard, Clarenmore was on some belated Grand Tour.

Not that Perth was jealous. Go off adventuring across another continent, sampling foreign food, drink, and women to his heart's content? Who the devil would want to do that?

All right, he was mad with envy.

Particularly given his current circumstance: trapped under the same roof for the next four weeks as four husband-hungry sisters and their equally starved friends. If recollection served, at least the middle Rosewood chit was pretty on the eyes. Or so the rumors went. Emily? Beatrice? He couldn't remember her name. Didn't know what any of them were called, except for the eldest. And that was only because he'd had the great misfortune of dancing with her once upon a time.

Lady Lavinia Rosewood.

Wait.

That wasn't right.

Lillith?

No.

Lenora.

It was Lenora. He was almost certain.

A stiff, somber creature with big blue eyes and a chin that had jutted out in disapproval for the entirety of their waltz. All because he'd generously complimented her lovely bosom. And it *had* been quite lovely. Just the right size, neither too big nor too small. The way the candlelight had glowed on all that soft porcelain skin…sheer perfection. You'd think she would have been pleased that he had noticed. Most women would have melted at such attention. But not Lady Lenora. That little wasp had turned right around and stung him before she'd stalked off, all self-righteous indignation and corset laces that were obviously tied too tightly.

"Please tell me they at least have decent brandy here," he told his mother in a lowered voice as they were escorted into the main foyer and through a wide hallway to the rear gardens where other guests milled amidst circular tables set with white linens and an assortment of meats, cheeses, and fresh fruit. A servant circled carrying a platter of champagne, and Perth neatly nicked a glass as the fellow went by. "Because God knows I'm not going to get by on this alone."

"Can you not behave yourself for one minute?" the dowager duchess asked mildly. Small in stature but not strength, Anastasia's serene countenance concealed a spine of steel. A spine that she'd needed to survive thirty years of marriage to a man who hadn't loved her for a single day. Who had taken pleasure in making sure that she knew it. Who had never forgiven her for not meeting his impossible expectations.

Where the late Duke of Monmouth had grown more gluttonous with each passing year, his jowls drooping, his stomach protruding, and his gout getting progressively worse, Anastasia had maintained her natural beauty. Her demure manner, delicate build, and blonde hair, now threaded regally with strands of silver, was what had attracted the duke to her in the first place, despite her being the third daughter of a baron without political ties or a dowry to speak of.

Their connection was immediate. Their chemistry palpable. One turn around the ballroom, and she was already smitten with the tall, dashing duke who said the most gallant things to her. Quickly–too quickly–they'd moved into a courtship, and then a proposal, and then a marriage.

By the time she realized that the handsome gentleman she had given her heart too was really a proficient actor with two mistresses on the side that he had no intention of giving up, it was too late. She was caught. A fox with her paw in the iron jaws of a trap. The more she pulled, the more she bled, until she came to the conclusion that the only way out was to be patient. To wait. To bide her time until her husband's lecherous life of excess caught up with him.

Which it had.

In spectacular fashion.

It saddened Anastasia that she saw some of Monmouth's traits in her one and only child. Perth was *not* his father. She'd made sure of it. He may have been callous, but he wasn't cruel. Quick to anger, but careful with his words when he did. Appreciative of the finer things in life, but not beholden to them. Yet he *was* undeniably charming. Even more so than his sire had been. And whether intentional or not, he'd already left a trail of broken hearts in his wake.

She hoped that by bringing him here, she might realize a wish that she and her dear friend, Lady Catherine Rosewood, had made when they were but girls at finishing school. A wish that when they were grown, and married, their children might meet and fall in love, effectively binding their two families together.

They'd tried when Catherine's eldest daughter had her debut, but their discreet nudging had ended in disaster.

Perth had been, well, Perth, and by all appearances Lenora hadn't taken to him in the slightest. Ironically making her one of the *only* women to be immune to his considerable charm.

Bridget, the second daughter, was far too shy and withdrawn. Catherine and Anastasia had unanimously agreed that she and Perth would never make a good match. And so they'd set their sights on Annabel. Beautiful, confident, and witty, she was sure to turn Perth's head and hopefully had the temperament to keep him in step. But then Catherine was lost, and her husband soon after, and the Rosewoods retreated into mourning.

This would be the first time Anastasia had seen Catherine's girls since the funeral. She had kept in correspondence with a letter at Christmas and another in spring, but words written to paper were hardly a substitute for meeting someone in the flesh. She was eager to spend the next month in their company. Sad, as well, for Catherine's daughters would surely be a bittersweet reminder of Catherine herself. Lenora especially, who was her mother's walking picture.

"I *am* behaving," Perth countered before he took a sip of his champagne. "This is me on my best behavior. Look, I'm even wearing trousers."

"I would like you to take this seriously." While Anastasia's voice was stern, her gaze was soft. Her son was her pride and joy. And while he undoubtedly had his imperfections, his flaws were not so large that a loving wife couldn't fix them. Because that was what he needed. Love. What he'd always secretly craved from his father. What she'd done her best to give him, but a mother was only capable of so much.

She still remembered, with heartbreaking clarity, when Perth was a young, impressionable boy of twelve. He had built a model boat out of kindling sticks, and even cut small pieces of canvas for the sails. She'd accompanied him into his father's study so that he might show off his hard work. All he'd wanted was a moment's acknowledgment. Even a nod would have sufficed. But the duke was in a mood, and he'd looked at the boat with such vile disgust that Perth's narrow shoulders had drooped before he even said a word.

"This is what you've been spending your time on?" Monmouth had sneered. "What does it do?"

"It is for display," Anastasia had intervened, desperate to save her son the pain of yet another disastrous encounter with his father. "Do you see the stitching on the sail? Perth did that himself with the use of a magnifying glass. Isn't he talented?"

Yes.

That was all the duke had to say.

One word, three letters.

*Yes.*

But that wouldn't bring him the satisfaction he was looking for. The satisfaction that came from asserting his dominance, his will, his control over someone smaller and more helpless than himself.

"Stitching?" he had repeated, his mouth curling a sneer. "Stitching is for girls. Are you a girl, Perth?"

"No," Perth had mumbled.

"Speak up, girl. I can't hear you."

Once again Anastasia had tried to come her son's rescue, but this time Perth had shrugged her away. Teetering between boyhood and that foreign notion of what it meant to be a man, he hadn't wanted to appear reliant on his mother.

"I'm *not* a girl," he'd said, his brown eyes flashing in a rare display of defiance.

"Give me the boat," Monmouth had demanded.

Perth hesitated. "But–"

"*Give it to me.*"

Hate had risen like bile in the back of Anastasia's throat as her son grudgingly handed over his boat. She knew what her husband was going to do even before he gave the wooden vessel a cursory study...and then threw it against the wall with all his strength.

Perth whined when it broke into pieces. A small, inadvertent sound. The same that a kicked dog might make. But it was just loud enough to cause Monmouth's head to swivel.

"Are you *crying?*" he'd said incredulously.

"No," Perth had denied even as he had swiped the cuff of his sleeve across his face, his lanky, half-grown body trembling from the strength it was taking to contain his emotions.

"You did not have to do that." Anastasia had known she was risking bringing her husband's ire onto herself, but what was a mother's job if not to take the blows intended for her child? "He's been working on that boat for weeks. All he wanted to do was show it you."

"Toys are for girls. Crying is for girls. All you're missing, Perth, is a skirt." Monmouth had jabbed his finger at the door. "Get out, both of you. Return when you're ready to behave like a son." His enraged gaze cut to Anastasia. "And you like a wife."

They'd left. She walking behind Perth with her head held high while he shuffled along with his chin pressed to his chest and his shoulders bowing beneath the weight of his father's perpetual disappointment.

Later that evening, she had waited for Perth in the library where she always met him after an episode with his father. They would enjoy warm apple cider and she would read his favorite book to him and yes, sometimes he would cry. In the safety and the comfort of his mother's arms, his bottom lip would wobble and his voice would crack as he asked her what he could do to make his father love him.

What *he* could do.

Because even at twelve, he'd already blamed himself.

But Perth never came. When she'd tiptoed into his bedchamber, she found himself fast asleep, his sweet brow troubled. She had smoothed the hair off his face, and pressed a kiss to his temple, and left the room, burdened by the suspicion that this time...this time Monmouth's thoughtless actions had done irreparable harm to a young child's impressionable spirit.

After that day, Perth had changed. Subtle changes that most wouldn't have recognized, but she wasn't most. She was his mother. And her heart had ached as she had watched her gentle, inquisitive boy grow into a hard, cynical man. His demeanor forged in the fires of constant disapproval and mockery.

Monmouth may have never bothered to teach his son how to ride a horse, or catch a fish, or shoot a pistol, but he had imparted one lesson before he died: if you hid your hurt behind a quick wit and sarcastic smile, no one ever need know how much pain you were in.

"I'm here, aren't I?" Perth finished his champagne and absently twirled the crystal stem between his fingers. "Although I still don't see why you couldn't have written a bloody letter."

"Language," she said, lightly tapping his arm in admonishment. "There are ladies present."

Perth grimaced. "Please don't remind me."

"Give it a chance, dear. The Rosewood sisters are lovely. They are intelligent, well read, and remarkably beautiful. Particularly Lady Annabel, whom I believe you will find much in common with."

He cast her a sideways glance. "And there it is."

"There is what?" she said, feigning ignorance.

"The reason you dragged me out here." Perth stopped and put a hand on his hip. "You're after making a match, aren't you? Well, let me be the first to tell you that this Annabeth chit–"

"Anna*bel*," she corrected.

"–could be a goddess sent from the heavens above and I'd still not be interested. How many times have I told you that I am not after a wife, Mother?"

Dozens.

They'd had this exact same conversation dozens of times.

Each more frustrating than the last.

"You have to marry eventually–" she began, but he cut her off with a snort.

"Says who? Pray tell, what law is written that says I *have* to marry?"

"Perhaps not a law, but decades–centuries–of Monmouth dukes have stood where you are. And every single one of them took a bride, or else you *wouldn't* be standing there."

"And how did that work out for them? By all accounts, each Duke and Duchess of Monmouth were more miserable in their marriage than the last pair. Yourself included. Why would I ever care to carry on that particular tradition? It would be the very definition of lunacy."

"For love," she said simply.

His brow furrowed, much as it had that night so long

41

ago when he'd laid asleep in bed, crushed by his father's maliciousness. Then he delivered a cutting laugh. "Love is a fairytale, Mother. You of all people should know that." For an instant, his countenance softened as he lowered his head and pressed his lips to her cheek in a chaste kiss. "I love *you*. I love my horse. I love my vintage bottle of Glenavon Scotch. That will have to suffice. Now if you'll excuse me, I need to find where that nice servant went with the champagne."

As Perth strode away, Anastasia found herself gazing up at the heavens.

*Not to worry, Catherine,* she vowed silently. *He may have gotten that sarcastic wit from his father, but his stubbornness is from me. And I'm not about to give up that easily.*

# 3

## *Champagne Problems*

THE HOUSE PARTY BEGAN as the last one had. With the early arrival of the Rosewood's neighbors, the elderly Lord and Lady Goldsmith. Far into their seventies, the viscount and viscountess had been attending the annual party since Lenora's grandparents were the ones hosting it. Lord Goldsmith was nearly deaf, Lady Goldsmith couldn't see two feet in front of her face, but together they formed an adorable example of what marriage was supposed to be like: a practical allegiance that had eventually blossomed into love.

No sooner had Lenora made sure that Lord and Lady Goldsmith were settled comfortably at a table in the shade, than the other guests started to arrive with alarming frequency. That, too, was familiar. The quiet and then the sudden rush of mayhem. Except this time it was Lenora, not her mother, who ushered friends and family through the foyer and out into the rear gardens where a reception luncheon would allow everyone ample opportunity to exchange pleasantries and sate their hunger before they retired to the rooms that had been prepared for them. A brief rest, a chance to change out of their traveling clothes, and then everyone would convene in the grand dining hall for dinner followed by whist in the drawing room for the ladies and cigars for the gentlemen out on the terrace.

Lenora milled about her guests with a smile fixed to her lips. She had traded her morning dress for a more formal gown of mossy green. Pinned tight at the hip, it hugged her ribcage before opening into a round skirt supported by crinoline, a hooped petticoat designed to emphasize the slimness of a woman's waistline. Ivory lace adorned the modest bodice and trailed from elbow-length sleeves while stripes of lighter green satin adorned the hem.

It really was a pretty dress. One of her best. But it was hot out, and the bustle was heavy, and she could already feel a trickle of sweat making its way down the middle of her spine.

Her mother had always made it seem so *effortless*. Greeting everyone, and remembering all their names, and seeing to their special needs, and making them feel as if they were the only people in attendance. She'd even memorized their favorite drink. And Lenora, who had presided over tea parties and picnics but never anything of such magnitude or importance, was already beginning to doubt her decision to have the house party again in the first place.

But she had to do it.

She *had* to.

If her mother were alive, it was what she'd want. What she'd expect. For her eldest daughter to one day fill her shoes and take over duties as hostess, freeing her to actually enjoy herself instead of running about for the benefit of everyone else. At least up until James took a bride, and it became *her* responsibility.

Except James wasn't here. And neither was her mother. Leaving Lenora to keep up appearances in their absence, scout out potential suitors for her sisters, and–most importantly–prevent awful Cousin Richard from suspecting anything was amiss.

Which meant this house party needed to run *flawlessly*.

"We're out of glasses, my lady." Pink faced and out of breath, Annie, a scullery maid, came rushing up out of nowhere. She was a sweet girl, if a tad daft and prone to fits of hysteria. She was also a recent hire, brought on to replace some of the half dozen or so staff that had retired due to age or illness or the want to be employed by a household that didn't have a cloud of bad luck hanging over it.

"Glasses?" Lenora said blankly. "How can we be out

of glasses?"

"The guests are…thirsty?" Annie ventured.

Lenora cast a discreet glance across the garden. Framed in by a thick patch of forsythia to the left and a stone wall covered in climbing roses to the right, the space had been designed to function as an outdoor extension of the main drawing room. Paths lined with white marble chips encouraged guests to explore the benches and fountains before winding inward to a gazebo screened for both comfort and additional privacy. Tables dressed in ivory linens and wildflower bouquets taken from Clarenmore's own fields had been set at random intervals, giving guests plenty of space to cluster together or spread out, depending on their preference.

At capacity, the garden could easily hold over a hundred people without appearing crowded, even though the twenty-one guests that had arrived thus far were more than enough. Four more were due tomorrow, including Cousin Richard, bringing the grand total to twenty-five.

Twenty-five…and they were already out of champagne glasses.

It was a disaster.

*No*, Lenora told herself sharply.

It was only a disaster if she let herself *think* it was a disaster.

And she wasn't going to do that.

She could not afford to do that.

"There are more glasses in the china cabinet in the east

wing hall. The cut of the crystal is slightly different, but hopefully no one will notice." She crossed her arms and drummed her fingers against her sleeve. "They may need a light dusting."

"Is the east wing by the library or the solarium?"

Lenora stared at the maid. "We do not have a solarium."

"Oh." Annie gave an anxious, high-pitched giggle that ended on a squeak. "That's right. I forgot. Apologies, my lady. It's a much larger house than the last one I served in, and I am still learning where everything is."

Annie had been employed at Clarenmore Park for six months, but Lenora had the sinking feeling that in six years the flustered maid would still be wandering into broom closets when she was looking for the kitchen.

"It's all right." Lenora's smile tightened at the corners, but remained in place. "I'll send someone else."

Except when she looked about, all of the other servants were busy assisting the guests and both the housekeeper, Mrs. Weidman, and the head butler, Mr. Barnaby, were inside ensuring that everyone's belongings were brought to the correct bedchamber and the dining room was being set for the receiving dinner–a seven-course meal that Cook had begun preparing before dawn–and any last minute emergencies were being attended to.

Lady Clarenmore had often commented that she knew a social function was successful when it resembled a duck gliding effortlessly across the surface of a pond…while its webbed feet paddled madly beneath. The analogy had never quite made sense to Lenora, but now she understood it enough to know that her duck was sinking.

"Not to worry," she said determinedly. "I shall fetch them myself."

"Should I accompany you?" Annie asked, wringing her hands.

"No. No, remain here. Circle about and collect any empty glasses you can find, then bring them straight to the kitchen to be washed." She paused. "You *are* aware where the kitchen is, aren't you Annie?"

The maid's head bobbed with such enthusiasm that her cap came askew. "Yes, my lady."

"Excellent." A final sweep of her gaze around the garden to ensure that Eloise wasn't hanging from a tree somewhere, and Lenora hurried inside, wanting to be in and out before her absence was detected and commented upon.

Narrowly avoiding crashing into a footman carrying an enormous tray of skewered shrimp tails, she kept to the side of the hallway as she made her way to the east wing. Now rarely used, this section of the house with its mahogany paneling and wide planked floorboards was original to the estate. The other parts, including the drawing room, matching front parlors, and west wing addition where the majority of the guests would be staying, had been added over the years.

Traditionally, the east wing was for family. It contained her father's study, her mother's music room, and their bedroom. Unlike most married couples, they'd slept together, even going so far as to knock down the wall between the lord and lady's separate chambers in order to make one big, inclusive space.

After their deaths, Lenora and her siblings had gradually drifted to the main part of the house. It wasn't a conscious decision, but rather one born of self-preservation. It had *hurt* to walk past the study and not see her father sitting as his desk poring over the week's ledgers, or to wander by the music room and wonder why the pianoforte wasn't singing with the sounds of Beethoven's *Fur Elise*.

To protect themselves, and their grieving hearts, they'd silently agreed to leave the rooms as they were when their parents were alive. No one was to use them or change them, and with the exception of the maids who cleaned or moments of quiet reflection, no one went in them, either.

Which was why she did a double take when she passed by her father's study and realized that not only was the door ajar, but someone was moving about within. A guest, most likely, who had gone in search of the water closet and gotten turned around.

"Excuse me," she said pleasantly as she pushed the door open wide and stepped into the study. The shades were drawn, the only light coming from an oil lamp on the desk that she'd ordered be kept lit at all times. It took a second for her eyes to adjust. When they did, she sucked in a startled breath. *"You."*

Perth Stewart, the Duke of Monmouth and the rudest, most offensive man she'd ever had the displeasure of waltzing with, was standing in the middle of her father's study holding a bottle of the late earl's brandy from his private collection.

A collection that no one was to touch, not even James.

And especially not Perth!

The cad.

Lenora had met quite a few self-entitled nobleman during her three seasons, but none worse than the Duke of Monmouth. He was, without a sliver of a doubt, the most arrogant, conceited, *insufferable* gentleman in existence. Worse yet, he was strikingly–obnoxiously– handsome. A fact that he knew full well, and one that did not help to curb his self-absorption in the slightest.

Tall and broad shouldered, he had the fair coloring of a Greek God and the dark eyes of a devil. His jaw was carved from granite, his chin from marble. His nose wasn't bulbous, as noses sometimes had a tendency to be on otherwise handsome men, but rather long and straight and proportioned to the rest of his face. The clothes he wore fit his muscular frame like a glove, the maroon silk velvet of his jacket bringing out the chips of amber in his gaze as he raked her derisively with it.

*"You,"* he said, his upper lip curling.

Surely it was a sin, Lenora decided, that such a fine example of masculine beauty had been wasted on a lout like Perth.

"Put that down at once," she demanded, driving her heel into the floor for emphasis. "What are you doing in here? This room is private."

"Looking for better swill than that watered down squash you're trying to poison us all with outside. *Obviously*," he drawled, arching a tawny brow.

Lenora forced herself to take a deep breath. It was either that, or pick up a book off the shelf and throw it at Perth's inflated head. But he was a duke. A *powerful* duke. And with three sisters to marry off, she could ill afford to have him as an enemy.

"Your Grace," she began in a voice so falsely sweet that it made her teeth ache. "I apologize if you have found the champagne lacking. But this is a private study, not intended for guests. If you would be so kind as to follow me out–"

"Someone should also tell you that the shrimp is rubbish," he interrupted. "And the oysters are at least a day past their prime. If you're going to serve seafood, best make sure that it's fresh."

A small book.

A small book wouldn't cause too much damage.

Why, it would hardly leave a bruise.

When her hand started to inch towards the shelf, she snatched it back and tucked the offending limb behind her, fingers curling into a fist with her thumb pressed in the middle. If she could coax Eloise down from a tree, then surely she could handle an ill-behaved, boorish lummox whose entire self-worth came from his title and that golden lion's mane atop his head.

He *did* have nice hair. A tad longer than the current style called for, but the choppily cut pieces framed his countenance nicely. She wondered if it would feel soft or coarse. Then immediately wondered *why* she was wondering.

It was this room.

It brought out all sorts of feelings in her. Emotions that she'd done her best to suppress these three years past, because emotions did not a good match make. If she wanted to successfully launch her sisters into High Society and save Clarenmore Park in the process, then she needed to remain as hard and unyielding as Perth's perfect jawline.

"I shall make our chef aware of your dissatisfaction," she said calmly. "In the meantime, I would be happy to accompany you back to the garden after you've returned my father's brandy."

Perth lifted the bottle and peered at the amber contents within. "This belonged to Lord Clarenmore?"

"Indeed." She made a gesture with her arm. "This is– was–his study. As I am sure you can imagine, it is closed to visitors."

To her surprise, the duke complied with her request

without so much as a snide remark.

"My apologies," he said after he'd carefully returned the bottle to the liquor cabinet, and she blinked when he even went so far as to lower himself into a bow. "I was not aware of the significance of this room when I entered it. I will not make the same mistake again."

"It's…it's quite all right." Lenora frowned. Rude, sardonic, arrogant Perth was easy to dislike. Loathe, really. But this person–whoever he was–invoked a completely different response. If she didn't know him better, she might have even…dare she think it…found his company somewhat *tolerable?*

Ew. No. Absolutely not.

"I was sorry to hear of the death of your parents," he went on, and it was all she could do not to gape openly. "As I am sure you are aware, our mothers were good friends."

"Yes, I am aware. They both went to the same academy. Her Grace has been kind enough to reach out to my sisters and me on several occasions. We have greatly appreciated her letters, and the thoughtful words within." Her thumb slid out from her palm as her fist slowly unfurled. "I, too, was sorry to hear of your father's death. To lose a parent before their time must be one of the most difficult things to endure in this world, second only to losing a child."

A muscle ticked in Perth's jaw. In the dim lighting, his eyes burned black. "Who said it wasn't his time?"

Her mouth opened. Closed. It wasn't often that she lost her composure. But Perth had managed to rob it from her twice in the past five minutes. "I–"

"Don't speak of what you don't know, Lady Lenora."

"I was merely passing on my condolences," she said stiffly.

"Keep them. They're not wanted."

Eloise would have thrown a book at his head by now, and a vase besides.

Annabel would have batted her lashes and had him half in love with her.

Bridget would have scampered from the room like a frightened rabbit.

But Lenora merely smiled. A polite smile. The kind that could slice straight through a person before they even realized they were bleeding.

"Your manners are a day past their prime, Your Grace. As such, they are beginning to emit quite a noticeable stench, and I fear I must excuse myself before my eyes begin to water. I trust, given how you found your way in here without instruction or permission, that you can manage to find your way back out."

Without permitting him the courtesy of a final word, she turned on her heel in a graceful flutter of green muslin and quit the room.

# 4

## *Insufferable Bastard*

SHE'D STUNG HIM again. As Perth stared at the doorway that Lenora Rosewood had just passed through, his brow furrowed. The chit had all the charm of a wasp whose nest had just been disturbed in the height of summer.

And damned if he wasn't a tad aroused by the pain.

As a reluctant grin laid claim to his mouth, he sauntered out of the study–had he known it belonged to the late Earl of Clarenmore, he'd never have entered, nor attempted to swipe a bottle of brandy–and returned to the garden. He cast a glance around for an ice queen with cobalt blue eyes and midnight black hair, but it appeared Lenora had not preceded him outside.

Pity, that.

He wouldn't have been averse to continuing their

sharp-witted banter. But it seemed that any more thinly veiled insults would have to wait, as he certainly wasn't going to go chasing after her like some sort of lovesick fool.

Perth didn't chase.

He *was* chased.

By every debutante, widow, and married woman in England.

And a few men besides.

Which was why there was a part of him–a sliver, really–that found Lady Lenora Rosewood somewhat intriguing. If only because she hadn't shown any inclination to throw herself at his feet in a dramatic display of love at first sight. Nor had she pretended to find him loathsome, when in truth she was merely playing hard to get.

No, Lenora *genuinely* despised him.

How utterly fascinating.

After ensuring his mother was comfortably engaged with two ladies of similar age, he took up occupancy on an empty bench that sat atop a slight knoll, affording him a view of the festivities in their entirety.

He recognized most–if not all–of the attendees. The Rosewoods and the Stewarts had long occupied the same elite social circles, and shared most of the same acquaintances.

There was Lord and Lady Greer, patrons of the arts whom had devoted their considerable fortune to the

British Museum. A noble pursuit, Perth supposed, if one did not have any vices or children to squander their fortune upon.

Given that he had no plans for the latter, he was deeply devoted to the former. So long as his mother and tenants were provided for, he had no qualms in wasting every last shilling on whisky and women. It's what his father would have *hated*. And Perth took great pleasure in envisioning the old man rolling in his grave each time he spent an obscene amount of money on a bottle of Glenavon Scotch.

Closer to the house, Lord and Lady Goldsmith were shouting at each other. Not out of anger, but rather because the elderly couple were as deaf as a couple of bats. A terrifying example of what sixty years of marriage did to a person. Although Perth's lips did twitch in amusement when he watched the viscount stuff a shrimp into his pocket.

The Marquess and Marchioness of Donegall were here with their two daughters, bland looking things with mousy brown hair and buckteeth.

There was a pair of Americans, who all but reeked of new money.

Lady Hatchett, a widow on the hunt for a new husband.

A loud Scot and his English bride, whose names escaped him.

Lord Croft, whom he had attended Eton with. Serious

fellow who had never joined his schoolmates at the local pub, and had preferred studying to cow tipping.

Just a few feet away, the Earl of Hensworth was sharing a glass of champagne with the giggling Lady Pratt. Their affair was widely known despite them both being married…and having both of their partners standing with earshot.

It might have been scandalous, if it wasn't so predictably boring.

As far as the *ton* was concerned, if you didn't marry for wealth or title and then seek your pleasure elsewhere, you were in the minority. Love matches were generally scoffed at, and it was never long before one, or both, parties began to stray outside the marital bed. Why go through the trouble of setting high expectations that were only ever going to end in inevitable heartache? Not to say that Perth would commit himself to a bride and then stray on *purpose*. But the lineage was there, wasn't it? The poor breeding that predisposed him to committing the same sins as his father.

Marrying for love was merely asking for trouble. It was bound to end in hurt feelings and contempt. By God, what if some sap married Lady Lenora because they fancied themselves in love with her? What a disaster *that* would be. Admittedly, it wouldn't be too difficult to be won over by those big blue eyes and silky black hair and high, high cheekbones. But anyone foolish enough to put a ring on the ice queen's finger was in for a world of disappointment once the rosy glow began to wear off and they froze to death in their own bed.

Frostbite in the nether regions.

That's what awaited Lenora's future husband.

Although wouldn't it be tempting to see what might happen to all that ice if it encountered a little heat?

"I did not think you would be here." Graham Northam, The Viscount Croft and heir apparent to the Earldom of Rutland, looked much as he had at Eton. A dour, grim-faced scholar trapped in the body of an aristocrat. On the rare occasions he'd joined Perth and his friends on a break from their studies to go carousing about town, the ladies had *swooned* over him. Perth had never understood it himself. Something about Graham's shoulder length brown hair and "piercing green eyes" and poet's soul, blah blah blah.

For his part, the viscount had rarely paid his admirers any mind. No fun, that one. Which explained why he and Perth, while amicable, had never been particularly close. Were they best mates, Perth would have almost certainly intervened when Graham announced his engagement to Lady Elsbeth Towley, a conniving bitch who had her eyes set on the shiniest prize she could get her greedy little hands–and mouth–on.

Graham, wet behind the ears and oblivious to the deceptive practices of certain females, hadn't stood a chance once Elsbeth had hooked her claws into him. She'd had him wedded and bedded within a year, and by the time he discovered what a cuckold she had made out of him, they'd two small brats to contend with.

Perth didn't know the whole story. Graham didn't talk about it, and he wasn't about to inquire into a man's weakest moments. All he *did* know was that Elsbeth had claimed their marriage to be a sham, applied for–and was awarded–an annulment (it helped when you had an affair with the magistrate), and ran off to marry some rich desert sheik, leaving Graham to raise their children alone.

It was a sad, unfortunate affair.

And an *excellent* example of why marriage needed to be avoided like the bloody plague.

"I am here being a dutiful son," Perth said, nodding at the dowager duchess. He glanced at the space beside him, a subtle invitation for Graham to sit, which the viscount accepted. "What are you doing here? House parties aren't your regular scene."

Graham stared straight ahead. "I need a wife."

"Excellent," Perth replied after taking a second to curb his surprise. Hadn't the man learned his lesson the first time around? Apparently not, the poor sod. "You can have mine."

"You don't have a wife."

"To my mother's absolute and eternal disappointment. Go on." He gave Graham a hearty slap on the shoulder. "You can pretend to be her son, and I'll be you, sitting here all glum and dreary reciting Shakespeare. We'll trade places and make everyone chuffed."

Graham gave him a cursory glance out of the corner of his eye. "You don't know a word of Shakespeare. Or have you forgotten who took your tests for you in Professor Hetrick's class?"

"In my defense, you enjoyed taking those tests. Don't deny it."

He did not. "Violet and Sebastian need a mother. I need someone to manage the household affairs so that I can concentrate on my research. Thus, I need a wife."

"So you've come to the house party to…"

"Find one," Graham supplied.

Perth grimaced. "Don't say you have your attention set on one of the Donegall chits. If you have any other children, they'll come out half beaver."

"Has anyone ever told you what an insufferable bastard you are?" Graham asked mildly.

"All the time. At this point it's a compliment, really." He stretched out on the bench and put his hands behind his head. "You don't need a wife. You need a governess. Hell, even a well behaved cocker spaniel would do the trick. How hard can it be to watch over two babies?"

"They're five and four."

"Exactly. Give them a blanket and a bottle and call it a day."

"Have you ever…no." Graham shook his head. "Never mind."

"What?" Perth asked.

"I was going to ask if you'd ever seen a five-year-old

child, but the answer is fairly obvious."

"Not up close. They're messy." He lifted his jacket to show the inside lining. "This is imported silk." A thought occurred, and his brows snapped together. "You haven't brought them *here*, have you? Sebastian and–what's the girl one called?"

"Violet. And no, they're spending the summer at Rutland Crossing with my parents."

"While you search for a wife," Perth surmised.

"Precisely."

"I won't pretend to understand why you've decided to shackle yourself again, but if you want my advice–"

"I do not," Graham said curtly.

"–best avoid Lenora Rosewood."

"Why is that?"

Perth's eyebrows rose. "Have you *met* her?"

"Yes." Graham adjusted his tie, a checkered ascot that he'd run through with a gold pin. "I found her to be polite and a pleasant conversationalist."

Perth nearly snorted.

Polite and pleasant? That was probably the same thing a male praying mantis thought right before the female ripped its head off and *ate it*. One of the few delightful tidbits of information that he'd retained from his schooldays.

"Well, you don't have the best judgment, do you?" he said, lowering his arms.

A vein pulsed on the side of the viscount's temple.

"That is why I intend to make a far better choice this time. For both myself and my children."

"I've heard not terrible things about the middle sister, Annabel," Perth offered generously. "Haven't seen her myself yet to confirm, but rumor has it she has the face of an angel and the tits of–"

Graham stood up. "There is already someone I have in mind, thank you."

"Who?" Feigned horror took hold of his expression. "Not Widow Hatchett. You can't be *that* desperate. She'd make for a good mistress, maybe. But not a wife."

"And what would you know about that?"

Perth shrugged. "I'm always weighing my options."

"Last I heard you were with an actress from that touring Spanish Troupe."

"Esmerelda," he said with the vaguest touch of wistfulness. "She was an acrobat, not an actress. The things she could do with her thighs–"

Graham held up his hand. "I'm sure I don't want to know."

"Our affair ended over a year ago. She was out of my bed more than she was in it." His mouth twisted in a rueful grin. "Turns out that a touring acrobatic troupe tends to travel quite a lot."

"Say that five times fast," the viscount said dryly.

Perth's grin widened. "Lord Croft. Was that an admittedly poor attempt at humor?"

"Sod off."

"Ah, if only I could. But it seems I'm stuck here, same as you." His gaze flicked to where his mother was still conversing with the other dowagers. "Albeit for *very* different reasons."

"You're not looking for a wife?"

"Why the devil would I go and do that?"

"The usual reasons. To have an heir–"

"I've a cousin, twice removed," Perth interrupted. "Nice chap. He can be my heir."

"To oversee the management of the household."

"You've just described my butler."

"To be a hostess for dinner parties and balls."

"I'll find another acrobat."

"What about daily companionship?"

"I'll get *two* acrobats. Why is everyone so concerned with my marital status, or lack thereof?" Perth wondered aloud. "I would make a shoddy husband. You know it, as well as my mother. Your time would be better spent warning the young maidens away rather than steering me towards them like a wolf to a herd of helpless sheep."

"Maybe you're right," Graham said, sliding his hands into his pockets. "Maybe you shouldn't marry."

This time Perth didn't try to contain his snort. "Exactly what I've been trying to–"

"Or maybe you haven't met the right person."

"That's awfully romantic for a man whose wife ran off with a sheik."

Graham's countenance hardened. "I let my heart

64

override my head. It won't happen again."

"You *just* told me you're here to find another wife."

"A motherly figure for Sebastian and Violet," the viscount corrected. "We wouldn't even share the same house. I'd put her in the country with the children, and conduct most of my work from my office in London."

Perth shook his head in bewilderment. "Why not hire a governess, then?"

"Because a governess can quit when she finds a frog in her bed."

"Alive or dead?"

"It was still croaking when I threw it back in the pond."

"That's not so bad."

"The next day it was a drawer full of worms."

"Dear God. You *do* need a wife. Best not tell her about the children until you've said your vows."

"Why do you think they're at Rutland Crossing?" Graham's gaze suddenly cut past Perth to a blonde woman walking through the middle of the garden. His shoulders stiffened. "If you'll excuse me, there is someone I need to speak with."

Graham went off to find his wife, while Perth went to find more champagne.

# 5

## *Turtle Soup and Dukes*

THE RECEPTION went well, my lady." Bree, Lenora's personal maid, smiled encouragingly as she helped her mistress change into a gown of sapphire blue for the welcome dinner.

Lenora sucked in a breath and wrapped her hands around a bedpost when Bree took hold of her corset laces and began to tighten them row by row.

"If by 'well' you mean I didn't have to pull Eloise out of a tree then yes," she wheezed. "I suppose it did."

"Everyone showed up. That's a good sign. Or so your mother would have said."

Lenora's smile was bittersweet. "Yes she would have, wouldn't she?"

If there was anyone who had known the Countess of

Clarenmore better than her children and husband, it was Bree. The kindly servant had attended Lady Clarenmore since her debut. When she died, it seemed only natural that Bree take up the same role for Catherine's eldest daughter.

She had proved to be a steady and comforting presence in a time of great turmoil, imparting words of wisdom at the most opportune moments. Words that Lenora's mother might have said, if she were still here. Although when it came to corset fastening, there was no denying that Bree was notoriously ruthless, and Lenora gasped when the maid gave one last yank.

"I'm sorry, my lady," she said, even though she didn't *sound* very sorry. "You could go without a corset, as your sister has chosen to do. With your excellent posture and trim waist, it wouldn't be difficult to maintain the illusion that you were wearing one. Nobody need ever know."

"Eloise is already half feral," Lenora said wryly, for it was obvious what sister Bree was referring to. "If she found out that I wasn't wearing a full set of undergarments, we'd soon find her marching about in trousers."

Bree clucked her tongue. "You needn't be a perfect example for your sisters to follow *all* the time."

"If not me, then who?" Lenora would have turned to look at her maid, but the boning in the corset restricted such free movement. "I am responsible for them. For filling the shoes that–that my mother has left." When her throat prickled, she firmly pushed her grief aside. Later, when the dinner was over and the guests were asleep and she was alone in her room, she would permit herself the luxury of a good cry. Until then, she needed to retain control. Of herself, of her surroundings, and of her sisters. "You know as well as I that she never would have gone without a corset, and took great pride in her flawless appearance."

"As she should have," Bree agreed. "Lady Clarenmore was renowned for her fashion sense. But if I may be so bold, my lady, you are not your mother. However much you may resemble her."

Was that intended as an insult, Lenora wondered, or a compliment?

She *knew* that she wasn't her mother.

Of course she knew.

Every time that Eloise rolled her eyes, or a new house bill arrived that could not be paid, or Lenora had to let another beloved staff member go, she was reminded that she was not the impeccable and much beloved Lady Catherine Rosewood, esteemed Countess of Clarenmore, for Lady Catherine Rosewood would never have allowed any of those things to happen. When she was alive, Clarenmore Park had run like a well-oiled machine. Three years after her death and it was coughing black smoke into the air and rattling as loudly as the ancient warm-air furnace in the cellar.

"Are you nearly done?" Lenora asked, ready to move

on from the subject at hand both literally and figuratively. "Dinner is to begin at seven o'clock sharp, and I need to be early to ensure that the seating chart is followed."

"Almost, my lady." Bree tied off the corset stays in a double knot that would practically take a pair of forceps to undo, and then motioned another maid forward to assist her with lifting the heavy crinoline. This one was noticeably larger than what Lenora had worn to receive her guests, but its size was necessary to fill out the hooped skirt of her gown.

She raised her arms above her head as the leather loops were fastened and the belt drawn snug around her waist. The gown itself came next, an elegant concoction of blue velvet that fit snugly across her bosom and ribcage before expanding out into a layered waterfall of silk chiffon and ivory rosettes used to pin the various tiers into place.

A real white rose was fixed to the side of her coiffure, its thorns trimmed away and petals dipped in wax to ensure they did not wilt before the night was through. That is, just so long as she made sure to avoid standing directly underneath a chandelier.

Pearls were placed at her ears and a matching choker was fastened around her neck. A subtle dusting of rouge on her cheeks, a slick sweep of kohl along her lash line (a homemade concoction of gum acacia, India ink, and rosewater), a dash of shiny beeswax upon her lips, and she was ready to join her sisters.

Annabel, resplendent in dusky pink with her golden hair secured to the side of her head in a dramatic tumble of curls that defied gravity itself, was waiting for her in the hallway and Bridget, demure in forest green, was at the bottom of the stairs. Notably missing was…

"Has anyone seen Eloise?" Trepidation lurked beneath Lenora's calmly spoken question. She needed this dinner to set the stage for what was going to be–what *had* to be– an exemplary house party. The best that the Rosewoods had ever put on. If their little sister mucked it up–

"Here I am!" Breathless, Eloise came running into the foyer, slid across the slick marble tile, and came to a halt in front of Lenora. "And I am even dressed," she said, as if it were some great accomplishment that she'd managed to put on the yellow gown Lenora had laid out in her chamber that morning.

"You've combed your hair," Annabel said approvingly.

"And put ribbons in it." A dimple fluttered shyly in Bridget's cheek as she smiled. "You look lovely, Eloise."

Lenora began to nod in agreement, before her gaze fell to the floor and then shot back up with no small amount of alarm. "Where are your shoes?" she demanded. "Eloise, you're not wearing any shoes!"

The redhead sighed. "I can't be expected to remember *everything*. Besides, they pinch."

Of all the ridiculous–

"Beauty isn't meant to be comfortable," Annabel

noted with a haughty flick of her wrist. "I am fairly certain I've a hairpin jammed in my skull but you don't see me complaining, do you?"

"I have an extra pair of dance slippers you can borrow," Bridget offered. "I think we're about the same size."

"My feet will be under the table," Eloise said airily. "No one will even notice."

"Everyone is going to notice," Annabel predicted.

"Please, Eloise." Lenora clasped her hands together in a pleading gesture. "For *once* in your life, just do as you are told. I haven't the time to argue with you."

"I should have stayed in the tree," Eloise grumbled as she pivoted on her stockinged foot and sulked up the stairs. Within minutes she was back, shoes in place, and the sisters made their way to the dining hall where Eloise's lack of proper footwear quickly became the least of Lenora's concerns.

"Oh no," she whispered, her heart slamming into the wall of her chest when she stopped short at the head of the elaborately set table. Servants dressed in black moved in and out between the chairs, some carefully filling crystal flutes with champagne while others set the first course, a simmering green turtle soup garnished with a decorative sprig of parsley.

"What is it?" Bridget asked, coming up beside her. "Have we run out of glasses again? That was a good thing, you know. To have run out. It means that people

71

were enjoying themselves. I've never attended a party where the guests bemoaned that there was too *much* to drink."

Sweet Bridget could always be counted on to put an optimistic spin upon whatever ill was currently plaguing the household. But in this instance, there was nothing she was able to do or say to improve Lenora's plight.

"No, it's not that." She glared at the place setting to the left of hers. "It's *him*."

Bridget's pale brows rose in confusion as she read the name engraved on the rectangular ivory placard resting behind the bowl of turtle soup. "The Duke of Monmouth?"

"His company is intolerable," Lenora hissed in a rare display of heated emotion. "And I have to endure an entire dinner seated beside him!"

In her haste to get dressed and ensure her sisters were suitably attired and that all was running smoothly, she'd forgotten. She'd forgotten that with her parents dead and her brother gone, *she* was the head of the household, and as such would be granted rights to the red velvet chair at the end of the table. The chair that her father had once occupied. That her brother *should* be occupying, if he were here. But he wasn't, and in his stead the obligation fell to her.

At least she had a welcome toast prepared.

The one thing she *hadn't* prepared for?

Sitting next to Perth for three hours.

Three *hours*.

When she'd hardly managed three minutes in the study before nearly succumbing to the urge to clock him over the head with the full volume set of *Lives of the Engineers* by Samuel Smiles. Which, it went without saying, was quite cumbersome.

What if Perth said something obnoxious and she lost control and stabbed him with a fork? The house party would be ruined before it had hardly begun, and her sisters' chance for a good match would be dashed.

Social death by utensil.

What a terrible way to go.

"Surely it won't be that awful," Bridget said soothingly. "What can His Grace do in a room filled with nearly two dozen peers? I am sure that everyone, including the duke, will be on their best behavior."

"Have you ever met the Duke of Monmouth?" Lenora said under her breath as the dining hall started to fill with guests. "He doesn't *have* best behavior."

Bridget's fingers twined anxiously together. "I have to find my seat, but if you want me to get Annabel–"

"No." She forced a smile. "No, I'll be fine."

And she was.

Right up until the Duke of Monmouth sauntered over, took note of his chair in relation to hers, and said with a smirk, "Couldn't resist me, could you?"

"My ability to *resist* you has nothing to do with it," she said, speaking out of the corner of her mouth as she kept her smile firmly in place for the benefit of anyone looking in their direction. "You know as well as I it is your rank that has you here, nothing else. Were it up to me, you'd be sitting at a table in Antarctica."

"Is that the place with the penguins?" Perth stepped behind her and pulled her chair back; an excellent display of gallantry that was ruined by the mocking amusement shining in the dark depths of his mahogany gaze. "I can never remember if they are in the southern hemisphere or the north."

"The majority of penguins are found south of the equator, with the exception of a new subspecies that Mr. Darwin recently discovered in the Galapagos."

"Your knowledge of fat flightless birds is impressive, Lady Lenora."

Her eyes narrowed. "It is called reading, Your Grace. Might I suggest you try it sometime? Perhaps you could begin with a book on proper etiquette."

"Do you not find me proper?" he asked, his breath fanning across the exposed nape of her neck and causing a quiver of feminine awareness to race down her spine.

It slid forward into her belly, filling her with a warm, confusing heat. Almost like a fever, except she wasn't sick, and the flush wasn't in her cheeks, but rather...rather lower. In that soft, slick, secretive place that no other hand had ever touched except for her own. Even then, she'd never dared anything more than few hesitant, ticklish strokes in the midst of a long, restless night. Light, fluttering pulses of her fingertips that had left her with a strange, unfulfilled ache. An ache that she'd not dwelled on, until this very moment.

It was because of Perth, she decided.

He was standing close.

*Too* close.

Obviously this–this temporary illness was all his fault.

They had held hands when they'd danced, bringing them closer than they were now. But somehow, having him behind her with only the chair to separate their bodies, felt far more intimate. Perhaps because she shouldn't have been feeling *anything*. Not for him, of all rogues. And certainly not here, of all places.

She was about to address the room, for heaven's sake!

And she was…she was damp.

Down *there*.

It was wrong.

*He* was wrong. Wrong and wicked for invoking this…this forbidden ribbon of arousal that was slowly winding its way through her body.

"Please take your seat." Her hand shot out and grasped her glass of champagne. Miraculously, she managed to lift it off the table without spilling its contents down the front of her gown.

"As you wish," Perth murmured. But as he turned to his own chair–whether by accident or dark design–his hand brushed across her bottom, stealing beneath the layers of taffeta that comprised her bustle to the rounded curve of her left buttock.

He didn't squeeze or pinch. Merely kept his palm there for the length of a heartbeat; long enough to silently communicate that it was no accidental embrace. He'd wanted to touch her, and he had. As if he had every right to do so. As if...as if she were some private plaything on display for his personal pleasure.

"Your *Grace*," she hissed, nearly bobbling the champagne. In the cozy glow of candlelight her cheeks shone a bright, shiny red. She could only hope that the guests attributed her blush to a natural fear of public speaking, and did not guess the truth: that as much as she wanted to hate Perth for his possessive command of her body, she didn't.

Truth be told, there was a part of her that enjoyed it.

There was a part of her that was *thrilled* by it.

And that made her blush even more.

"My apologies, Lady Lenora." Perth's low, rumbling voice was for her ears only as he finally sat down. "You had a piece of lint just there on your skirt. I couldn't let a loose string mar such glorious perfection."

She didn't need to look at him to know that he was grinning. Like Lucifer himself, the Duke of Monmouth offered nothing but sinful temptation, and pity the poor soul foolish enough to succumb to his devilish delights.

"I shall speak with my maid," she said evenly, "to ensure that there is *never* a loose stitch to be found on my gown again." Dismissing him with an icy flick of her gaze, she turned her attention to the rest of the table. Awash in conversation, no one appeared to notice that she was finally ready to address the room.

Bridget was engaged in conversation with Perth's mother, the Dowager Duchess of Monmouth, while Annabel charmed Mr. Henderson, their American visitor who was keen on purchasing some of their father's breeding stock. In the middle of the table the Earl of Hensworth was exchanging a terse word with his wife as Lady Pratt sat across from them and pretended not to listen. The Dowager Blakely was almost asleep in her soup. Eloise had helped herself to the bread platter. Lady Hatchett was attempting to attract the focus of Lord Croft, and Angus McDougal, Laird of Glencairn, was entertaining the rest of the guests with a loud, boisterous tale about a wild boar that he'd captured with his bare hands while his young wife looked on with tender amusement.

"Here," said Perth, handing her his spoon. "Try this."

She snatched the sterling silver utensil out of his hand, then tapped the edge against the stem of her crystal flute.

The first tap yielded no results.

On the second, Eloise paused in stuffing her face with bread.

By the third, Lenora had gained nearly everyone's undivided attention.

Including Perth's.

She could *feel* him staring at her.

The searing weight of his gaze was as palpable as his hand upon her derriere.

Devil, indeed.

"I'd like to thank you all for gathering here today," she began, secretly relieved that her steady voice did not betray the tumultuous storm of emotion warring within her breast. "Our great-great grandfather started this tradition, and I know that he, along with our grandparents and parents, would be pleased to know that it is one that my sisters and I, and our brother, when he returns, plan to carry on." Her arm trembled ever-so-slightly as she raised her champagne; the only indication that beneath the surface of her calm exterior her nerves were fraught with tension.

Even without the added complication that the Duke of Monmouth provided, this would have been a difficult–if not impossible–speech to make. All things being equal, she'd have vastly preferred to be anywhere else but at the head of the table, in the spot that belonged to her father, and if not him, then her mother, and if not her, then James.

The very act of her standing in their place solidified the fact that they weren't here.

But as she'd told Bree…if not her, then who?

Bridget, Annabel, and Eloise were all looking at her with the expectation that she was going to say the right thing, do the right thing, be the right person. Because she was Lenora. Lenora, the eldest. Lenora, the peacekeeper.

Lenora, the one who held them all together even when she was on the brink of falling apart.

But they could never know that.

*No one* could ever know how perilously close to the edge she really was.

Not even herself.

"I-I hope that you find the next three weeks enjoyable," she continued. When the corners of her mouth started to hurt from smiling, she simply smiled all the more. "We've put together a wonderful itinerary of activities, but mostly my sisters and I are grateful for your company. May we use this time to honor old traditions, to remember those who we have lost, and to create new memories."

"Here, here!" Laird Glencairn shouted.

In unison, the guests lifted their flutes of champagne and clinked them together.

Lenora gave a subtle nod, and servants immediately filed in to distribute the second course, butter braised rack of lamb with roasted asparagus and apricots. Within minutes the room resounded with the sounds of silverware and conversation, signaling a successful beginning to what she prayed would be a successful house party.

"Well done," Perth commented as she slid weakly into her chair. He toasted her glass, then lifted a brow. "If you're not going to drink that, slide it over here. I need something to get through the next two hours of mindless drivel, and this dead sheep isn't going to do it."

Belatedly, she realized she'd forgotten to take a celebratory sip of her champagne along with the rest of the crowd. Snatching the flute out of Perth's reach, she closed her eyes, tipped back her head, and drained the bubbly liquid in a single long swallow.

"What?" she said defensively when she opened her eyes to discover that he was *still* staring at her, albeit with an expression of…concern? Surely not. To the best of her knowledge, Perth was incapable of empathy. "Are you not the only one who can drink to excess when the moment calls for it?"

"If that's drinking to excess, then I'm going to need a different word for whatever it is that I do. Another," he said, lightly snapping his fingers at a passing footman. "Your lady will have another glass of champagne."

"I won't," Lenora protested even as a flute materialized in front of her.

"Oh, go on," he said, using his knife to cut off a thin slice of lamb. "No one's paying any mind to you. Even if they were, it's a glass of champagne." He speared the lamb with his fork and lifted it to his mouth. "Not a bedroom in a brothel."

She was grateful she *hadn't* taken a sip of champagne, for surely in that second she would have spat it across the table.

"Your *Grace!*" How many times, she wondered irritably, would she say those exact same words with the exact same emphasis? Might as well stop now and save herself the breath, as they clearly were not having any effect.

"What?" Thoroughly unperturbed, Perth ate his first piece of lamb and went to cut another. "All I am saying, is that there are worse vices."

"I am sure you are familiar with all of them." Lenora's appetite had abandoned her halfway through her speech, but wanting to keep up the pretense of eating, she began to quarter her asparagus into three even rows of four.

Perth's teeth, straight and white save for a slightly crooked incisor that only added to his roguish appeal, flashed in a grin. "Intimately." Fork in one hand and knife in the other, he leaned towards her. "It would serve you well, Lady Lenora, to loosen those corset laces once in a while," he said in a low, husky voice that had her thighs clamping together under the table. "When a thread is strung too tightly, I've found it has the tendency to grow brittle and snap."

"And when a thread is strung too loose," she responded coolly, "I yank it out and dispose of it accordingly. Enjoy the rest of your meal, Your Grace."

With that, she purposefully switched to the dinner partner on her right. A direct breech of the social etiquette that she held in such high regard, but desperate times called for desperate measures.

"Lady Goldsmith, how are you finding the lamb?" she inquired politely.

"WHAT?" the elderly woman yelled, pointing at her ear. "Speak up, my dear. I can't hear you."

"SHE CAN'T HEAR YOU," Lord Goldsmith provided helpfully.

Perth snorted into his empty bowl of turtle soup.

Ignoring him, Lenora just smiled and repeated her question.

# 6

## *Two Peas in a Pod*

THAT WAS *EXHAUSTING*," Eloise groaned as she collapsed onto a sofa and let her head fall onto the padded armrest with an audible *thud*.

"It's true that we haven't entertained in a long while." Taking a more practical approach to her seating arrangements, Bridget perched on the edge of a chair and began to twist her long blonde hair into a braid. "I forgot how much talking is required."

"Well I, for one, had a *wonderful* time," Annabel sang as she sailed into the private sitting room that all of the sisters shared, a silk wrapper draped loosely over her shoulders.

Unique in design, the Crescent Room (as it was commonly known amidst family and staff) was in the shape of a half circle with a large window framed in velvet curtains overlooking the rear gardens, and comfortable chairs and chaise lounges scattered throughout. Four doors led to their individual bedchambers (the fourth belonging to James), and since they'd been dressed in pinafores, the siblings had often gathered here at the end of a long night to spy out the window at the adults, or tell ghost stories, or, as they grew older, enjoy a bottle of mulberry wine stolen from the cabinet reserved for the parties that they weren't yet allowed to attend.

Once a room for storage, and then an art studio for their grandmother, and then a nursery for James and Lenora before the subsequent arrivals of Bridget, Annabel, and Eloise demanded a much bigger space, the Crescent Room had undergone many renovations over the years, but had finally found its purpose as a gathering place for the Rosewood sisters to rest and unwind, either together or individually, at the end of a long day. And there was no day longer than one that began with skewered shrimp in the gardens and ended with a competitive game of whist in the drawing room.

"I thought Lady Pratt was going to toss her wine in my face when I won the last round," Eloise huffed. "Can you believe she accused me of cheating?"

"You *were* cheating," said Annabel.

"Yes, but it was for the common good."

"How is cheating for the common good?" asked

Bridget, her fair brow furrowing.

Eloise shoved a springy red curl impatiently behind her ear as she sat up on her elbow. "If I hadn't ended the game then, we'd be still be playing. I did us all a favor. You're *welcome*."

"Lenora, what do you think?" Bridget asked.

"Hmm?" Standing in front of the window, Lenora had only been half-listening to her sisters, her thoughts preoccupied by a far more sinister entity than Lady Pratt. Namely, the Duke of Monmouth. She'd not spoken another word to him during the dinner or after it, but he'd stayed on her mind all the same, like a nightmare that she couldn't escape even after waking.

She was annoyed by her reaction to him. By her *body's* reaction to him. Lust in and of itself was not a foreign concept. She was twenty-four, not fourteen. She...she knew things. Mostly second-hand, but she'd been kissed!

Once.

She'd been kissed once.

And even though the experience had been akin to having the tongue of a cold, wet, dead fish plunged into her mouth, it still counted.

All that to say, she wasn't some squirming, wide-eyed schoolgirl that thought babies appeared under cabbage leaves. She knew how sexual intercourse worked. The basic mechanics of what went where, anyway. She knew that unbridled passion had ruined more than a few reputations. And she knew that she wanted absolutely nothing to do it.

Or with Perth.

When she married–*if* she married, as there was no guarantee at this point–it would be for reasons far more important than desire or lust. She and her future husband would be compatible on a number of levels, including socially, economically, politically, and morally. If there was an attraction between them, all the better. But it was not going to be the driving force in making quite possibly the most important decision of her life.

"Bridget wants to know your opinion on cheating for the common good." Eloise abandoned her elbow perch and slid forward, so that her head hung upside down, while simultaneously hooking her legs over the back of the sofa.

It was a decidedly *un*ladylike position, but Lenora had learned to pick and choose her battles.

"Cheating of any kind, for any reason, is a poor show of decency." She gave her youngest sister a quick, conspiratorial smile. "But had you not ended the game when you did, I do suspect we'd still be in the parlor listening to Lady Goldsmith snore."

"See?" Eloise said triumphantly. "Common good trumps honesty."

"That's not what I–"

"You and the Duke of Monmouth seemed to be getting on well," Annabel cut in. Resting on the edge of a chaise lounge, she crossed her legs at the knee and leaned back onto her hands.

"Why…" Lenora paused to clear her throat when it went dry. "Why do you say that?"

"Because of the way you were conversing at dinner." She fussed with the lay of her wrapper. For Annabel, appearances were everything. Even when in the presence of her sisters. "Like peas in a pod, the two of you. He's very handsome, isn't he?"

"Very," Bridget agreed, then blushed.

"He's not hideous," Eloise said, which for her was quite generous, as she rarely commented on any man's physical appearance aside from remarking upon the number of hairs sticking out of his nose or the size of a facial mole.

"His Grace and I did exchange a few words," Lenora said cautiously. "But I would hardly describe us as two peas. He is a guest. I try to make it a point to speak to *all* of our guests. I had a pleasant conversation with Lady Goldsmith–"

"Didn't you say that you danced with him once?" Annabel interrupted again. "The Duke of Monmouth. During your first Season."

"You *did?*" Bridget gasped. "You never told me that."

"Because there was nothing to tell. It's getting late," she said briskly, changing the subject. "Cousin Richard is arriving tomorrow. We should–"

"What does he smell like?" Eloise asked.

"What does he *smell* like?" Annabel repeated. "What an odd question."

Bridget gazed at Eloise in concern. "I think you need to sit up. Your face is turning red. All the blood is rushing to your head."

"It's not an odd question, and I'm fine." But with a grunt, Eloise did roll herself back onto the sofa. "How a man smells is very important. You don't want to be married to someone who stinks like a pig sty, do you? Or one that wears women's perfume."

Lenora paled. "No one is marrying anyone, least of all the Duke of Monmouth."

"I thought you *wanted* us to get married," Annabel reminded her.

"No. I mean yes, I do. But–"

"A duke would be a splendid catch," said Bridget.

"Yes, a duke would. But not *this* duke."

"Then he does smell," Eloise said seriously. "I knew it. All the handsome ones do."

"No, he doesn't smell." Exasperated, Lenora threw up her arms. "He's just…just…"

"Just what?" Annabel asked.

"Intolerable," she snapped. "He is in*tolerable.*"

Her sisters exchanged a meaningful glance.

"What?" She lowered her arms. "What is it?"

"We've never seen you this emotional over a man before," Bridget said gently.

Eloise's nose wrinkled. "It's strange."

"It's not *strange*." Annabel beamed at Lenora. "She's holding a tender for him, that's all."

Perth?

They thought she was a holding a tender for *Perth?*

"Absurd," she scoffed. "I cannot stand him."

Another glance was shared, this one longer than the last.

At her wit's end, Lenora marched across the room to her bedchamber. "I'm going to sleep," she declared, the corners of her mouth jutting in a mulish frown. "I suggest you all do the same, as it's clear that the champagne has addled your minds. Monmouth is *not* a suitable candidate for a husband. For *any* of us. He is a scoundrel, and a ne'er-do-well besides. I'd like you to avoid him for the duration of his stay here."

Annabel's head tilted slyly to the side. "But I thought we should make it a point to speak to all of our guests?"

"Not this one!" Yanking open her door with a burst of temper that was far more suited to Eloise, Lenora slammed it shut behind her, effectively ending any further discussion involving the Duke of Monmouth.

IN THE WAKE of their elder sister's abrupt departure, the three remaining Rosewoods stared at each other with eyes wide and mouths agape. None of them had ever witnessed Lenora in such a state before. She was normally the sensible sibling. The voice of reason. The calm to their chaos.

"Have you ever seen her slam a door like that?" Bridget asked in a hushed tone.

"Never," Eloise replied, sounding impressed. "She was quite good at it. The trick is to start slowly, and then pull it in quick at the last second. That makes the most impact."

Annabel went to a side table and poured herself a glass of water from a ceramic pitcher. She lifted the glass to her lips, but didn't take a drink. "I believe it's plain what is happening here."

"Lenora has finally abandoned all hope of turning us into respectable members of High Society?" Eloise ventured hopefully.

"No." Annabel sipped her water. "She has fallen in love."

Bridget gasped. "With who?"

Eloise rolled her eyes. "I'd tell you to get your nose out of a book, Bridge, but for once you're not reading one."

"Monmouth." Another sip, and then Annabel set the glass aside and smoothed a crease from her wrapper. "She's fallen in love with the Duke of Monmouth. *Obviously.*"

"It wasn't very obvious to me." Frowning, Bridget tied off her braid with an orange ribbon and swung it behind her back. "Lenora said that he was intolerable."

"That doesn't mean anything," said Eloise. "*All* men are intolerable."

Annabel raised a finger. "The question, what are we to do about it?"

"Cousin Richard will be here tomorrow," said Bridget, and at once all three of their faces contorted in a grimace of mutual disgust. There was no love lost between the cousins. Since they were children, Richard had been pinching, shoving, and lying to get his way. As an adult, not much had changed. "We shouldn't do anything that would cause a ruckus, or draw undue attention."

Eloise's eyebrows wiggled. "Undue attention is my middle name."

"No, Bridget is right," said Annabel. "We must be discreet."

"What are we going to do?" Bridget asked.

"What *are* we going to do?" Eloise echoed.

Annabel's sigh was both long and suffering. "Have the Duke of Monmouth propose marriage to Lenora before the end of the house party, thus ensuring we are protected from Cousin Richard while launching us back into High Society as diamonds of the first water. *Obviously.*"

# 7

## *Between a Cock and a Hard Place*

PERTH ROSE UNCHARACTERISTICALLY early.

Not by choice.

Given *his* way, he'd have slept until noon.

It was the damned rooster. Cock-a-doodle-doing right under his bedroom window. And while he had no way to prove it, he was almost certain that Lenora had something to do with the feathered cock running amok. He didn't trust those cool blue eyes of hers. Framed by thick black lashes that curled at the ends, they were almost *too* beautiful. And beautiful things were notorious for being sharp; just look at the flower with which the Rosewoods shared their name.

A rose was a stunning work of nature. All those soft, velvety petals folding in on each other. And he *did* have a penchant for soft, velvety petals. But if you weren't careful, you'd lean in for a sniff and leave with a bloody finger.

Or in this case, a rooster crowing to the high heavens fifteen feet beneath your pillow.

"An axe," he said grimly as he shoved his feet into a pair of polished Hessians. "I need an axe."

"An axe, Your Grace?" Jacobson, a short, burly man with brown eyes and thinning hair, had been Perth's personal valet for five years, and in that period of time he'd grown accustomed to his employer's unusual demands.

Wine at two in the morning.

Readying the carriage for an impulsive trip to Bath at midnight.

Chasing a swan out of Perth's bed while pretending not to notice the nimble bodies sprawled atop him.

All things considered, an axe at half past seven was a perfectly normal request.

"Yes. The sharpest you can find. There's a cock I need to murder." With that dire proclamation, Perth quit the bedchamber and stalked downstairs.

Sunlight beamed in through the stained glass windows above the main entrance, painting the foyer tiles in a mural of blues and greens. It might have been pretty, if his mood wasn't so foul. Raking a hand through his hair, still damp from the water he'd splashed on his face upon waking, he entered the parlor and snatched up an apple from an array of colorful fruit displayed on a long sideboard along with an assortment of muffins, oat cakes, and scones. Put out for the early risers, he assumed. Of which now he was one, albeit not of his own accord.

"An axe, Your Grace." Jacobson appeared in the doorway, his countenance impassive as he held out the weapon that Perth had requested.

Perth took hold of it. "This is a butcher knife, Jacobson."

"You did not specify how large the cock was that you are slaying, Your Grace."

He bit into his apple, then dropped it into the pocket of his burgundy frock coat. "I suppose it'll suffice. Blade appears sharp enough. Yes," he said on a hiss of breath when he pressed his thumb against the pointed tip and a drop of blood welled. "This will do. Excellent job as always, Jacobson."

The valet placed his arms behind his back. "Do you require further assistance, Your Grace?"

"If a man can't handle a cock, then he's not much of a man, is he? Or so my father would have said." Perth's mouth twisted in a humorless smile. "I'll be fine, Jacobson. Nothing to it. Quick chop, and my days of rising with the dawn will be over, thank God."

He passed Graham on the way out. "Rooster woke you as well, did it? Not to worry. The wretched beast isn't long for this world."

"What rooster?" asked Graham, moving past him to the sideboard. Taking a plate, he began to slather jam onto an oat cake.

Perth blinked. "You mean to say you're awake on *purpose?*"

"I've been awake," the viscount corrected. "I like to begin my day with a rigorous five mile walk at sunrise."

"Are you ill?" If he was, Perth dearly hoped that it wasn't contagious. "Because I know of an excellent doctor in London–"

"I exercise for my health and peace of mind."

"Sounds awful."

Graham started to take a bite of his oat cake. Paused. "What are you doing with that?" he asked, nodding at the knife that Perth was holding.

"My civic duty. You can thank me later." Not wanting to wait around for more guests to start milling about (another reason he avoided early mornings: the kind of people who *did* enjoy them were distastefully chatty), he exited via a side door to avoid the foyer entirely. It brought him to a path carved from slabs of limestone that he followed around the edge of the manor until he found him.

His feathered nemesis.

A tall, colorful rooster with a regal head boasting a bright red comb and wattles, beady eyes, and blackish green tail feathers that lifted in defiance when it spied Perth.

Swallowing hard and immediately rethinking his actions, Perth took a step back as he tried to remember if chickens could fly. He certainly didn't recall them being so bloody enormous. The damned thing was the size of a dog! And were those *talons* sprouting out of the back of its legs?

"Easy there, my good fellow," he said, lifting the butcher knife when the rooster fluffed its wings. "Let's discuss this as gentlemen, shall we? If you could kindly lay your neck upon that rock over there, this will be over and done with before you can say chicken dumplings."

The rooster scratched the ground and then lowered its head into charging position. With its wings lifted and its chest puffed out, it was as terrifying a cock as Perth had ever encountered. And he'd once (completely by accident) seen Lord Goldsmith naked.

"Clearly there's been a mistake." He slowly lifted his arms in a gesture of surrender. "Mine, not yours. This wasn't the way to go about it at all. I see that now. If we could part as friends–"

"Your *Grace!*" a feminine voice squealed. "What are you *doing?*"

Perth groaned.

Not her.

Anyone but her.

He didn't have to turn around to know that it was Lenora charging up behind him. He'd recognize that disapproving tone anywhere.

"Nothing," he said casually. "Just out for a walk."

"You're holding an-an axe." Putting her hands on her

hips, she tipped slightly forward, affording him an excellent view of her bosom as she stopped beside him to catch her breath. Creamy white with a hint of gold from the sun, her breasts threatened to spill from her lace-trimmed bodice.

Be a shame if no one was there to catch them.

"It's a butcher's knife, actually. I did request an axe, but my valet was unable to procure one." With a degree of effort, he dragged his gaze up from those tantalizing globes to find her glaring at him.

"Might I remind you that my face is up here," she said icily.

"I like staring at your breasts better. They can't scowl at me."

Her mouth opened. Closed. Straightening, she muttered something undecipherable under her breath. He wasn't positive, but it sounded like, *"It's too early in the morning for this"*. Then she focused her attention on the knife he was still holding. A line of confusion notched itself between her ebony brows before her gaze traveled past him to the rooster and her eyes widened.

"Are you attempting to *murder* Sir Kensington?" she demanded.

"That insufferable creature has a name?"

"Answer the question, Your Grace."

"I wasn't going to murder the cock," he said, a tad offended that she'd think so little of him. "I was just going to silence him. By cutting off his head."

"That is the very definition of murder!"

"You're pretty when you're angry," he noted.

And she was.

All pink cheeks and eyes flashing with blue fire and a full bottom lip trembling with indignation.

What would that lip taste like if he sank his teeth into it?

Lust struck him hard and fast; a one two punch to his chest and gut that stole the air from his lungs and left him reeling.

Perth was used to being attracted to women. All shapes, sizes, and hair colors. Give him a blonde or a brunette, it didn't matter. Give him a blonde *and* a brunette, well, that was just a recipe for a good time. But his attraction generally did not extend below the surface. To have such a visceral reaction...to *this* woman in particular...it caught him off guard. Worse than that, it temporarily stripped him of his natural defenses, leaving him exposed and vulnerable.

Two things he swore he'd never be again.

They stared at each other, Perth incapable of producing a witty remark and Lenora too furious to respond to his last one. He considered kissing her. Of plunging his hands into all of that perfectly pinned hair and ravishing her mouth until she was writhing against him in helpless abandon.

He'd quite like to see prim, proper Lenora Rosewood writhe.

But there was an invisible line between them. Just there, in the grass. And he instinctively sensed that if he made the decision to cross it, he'd have no easy way of finding his way back.

Kissing Lenora would be no minor dalliance. She wasn't a barmaid looking for a quick tup and an extra piece of coin, or a bored wife in search of a randy young buck between her thighs, or a widow seeking a wealthy benefactor in exchange for an affair of discretion.

No, Lenora was a lady. Through and through. A lady in want of a good husband. A kind, decent chap who dutifully dimmed the candles and ducked under the covers before conducting their prescheduled monthly intercourse.

A pity, as such a dodder wouldn't put that blue fire in her eyes.

But such was the price to be paid for mediocrity.

If Perth ever had her in *his* bed…if he ever had her in his bed, he'd light every bloody candle in the house. There wouldn't be an inch of that gorgeous skin he didn't want to explore. A single place on her body that he didn't want to lick. And therein laid the problem. Because a kiss *would* lead to fucking. Glorious, hot, passionate fucking. On the bed. Against the wall. Atop the damned dresser. After experiencing that clench of desire in his gut, he knew it as much as he knew his own name. But Lenora was not a woman to be fucked and forgotten. Once he had her, he'd have to marry her. Without question. He might have been a rake and a reprobate, but he did have *some* morals. They were weak and easily coerced, but they were there. And given that he had no interest in marrying at the current time, and he *definitely* had no interest in marrying an ice queen, he needed to be keeping his distance from the likes of Lenora Rosewood.

No more stealing a feel of that lovely, lovely arse at dinner. Work of art, that arse. Belonged in a museum, really.

No more getting distracted by her breasts.

No more saying the most outlandish thing he could think of just to see those high arching cheekbones fill with color.

When he was around Lenora, he needed to be the one thing he was not: a gentleman.

Or else the consequences would be dire for them both.

"All right, I will permit Sir Kensington's head to remain attached to his body," he said graciously.

"You'll *permit*–"

"So long as he commits to doing his morning salutations elsewhere."

On an exasperated huff of breath, Lenora crossed her arms beneath her breasts. Which only served to push them higher.

*Don't look,* he ordered himself. *Don't look, don't look, don't*–

Oh, bloody, blast, and damn.

He wasn't a saint, was he?

"Your *Grace!*"

"You keep saying that as if it's going to magically cure me of my wicked behavior. It's not," he said regretfully. "I've tried. It's no use."

"Try harder," she said through gritted teeth. "And give me that knife."

"Ladies shouldn't play with sharp things."

"Nor should they be subjected to the whims of arrogant men, yet here we are. Knife." She held out her hand, palm facing upwards. "*Now.*"

"Are you always this domineering?" he wondered as he gave it over handle first.

"Are you always this imperious?" Wielding the knife with great care, she went to the nearest window and rapped her fist upon the pane. A maid opened it, her scullery cap indicating that she was from the kitchens, and whisked the knife away with nary a blink.

"Yes," he said without hesitation once the window had closed. "It's one of my strengths."

Lenora smiled thinly. "Do you have a sewing needle, You Grace?"

"How the devil are we going to kill the rooster with a sewing needle?"

"We're not. But we *will* need something to pop the air in your head once you begin floating up into the clouds."

"Ah. I see." He scratched his chin. "Very amusing."

It was also supremely entertaining, not that he was going to tell *her* that. When was the last time he'd verbally sparred with a woman? Or anyone, for that matter? Not since before his father's death. It was as if once he'd been crowned with the title of duke, his peers went out of their way to treat him with the utmost respect and reverence.

Nothing he said was ever wrong.

Nothing he did was ever incorrect.

He could say the bloody sky was purple and his peers would smile and nod and agree with him. But not Lenora. The raven-haired beauty had no qualms about using that waspish tongue of hers to sting. She wasn't trying to impress him or curry his favor. He was even beginning to suspect that she didn't *like* him. Which was laughably absurd, of course. All women *loved* him. It was a tad suffocating, to be honest. The fawning looks. The mindless adoration. The simpering smiles.

So many simpering smiles.

Maybe that was one of the reasons why he found Lenora so...refreshing.

Or maybe he was merely lightheaded from being roused out of bed at the crack of dawn.

"You *are* going to have do something about that ferocious beast," he said with a nod towards the rooster. "I cannot be woken up before breakfast. It's bad for my health."

"Sir Kensington is not ferocious." Casting him a withering stare over her shoulder, Lenora walked up to the rooster and–much to Perth's disbelief–scooped it right up into her arms. The giant bird closed its eyes and nestled into her bosom as she stroked its neck, forcing Perth to come to terms with the uncomfortable realization that he was jealous of a cock.

*He* wanted to be pressed against those remarkable tits.

Dear God.

What was *happening* to him?

More importantly, how did he fix it?

"Oh no," Lenora said softly, her head swiveling in the direction of the tree-lined drive as a carriage pulled by a team of matching bays came rolling up, trailing a smoky veil of stone dust in its wake.

"What is it?" He'd never seen that look in her eye before. She almost appeared...resigned. As if she'd lost a battle before even lifting her sword. And he didn't like it. Not one damned bit. If anyone was going to defeat Lenora, it was bloody well going to be him. Not whoever was inside that carriage.

Without thinking, he reached out and touched her arm. Then immediately snatched it back when Sir Kensington pecked him on his wrist.

"Your damned rooster attacked me!"

"You were going to cut his head off with a butcher knife," Lenora replied without taking her gaze off the carriage. "I believe he's allowed. Here. Make amends."

She thrust the rooster at him then hurried off, leaving Perth with an armful of cock and a heart filled with confusion.

# 8

## *Besotted Musk Ox*

WHILE LENORA HURRIED to greet Cousin Richard, she silently and repeatedly cursed Perth under her breath.

The nerve of him! When she'd first spied the duke out of the corner of her eye as she was returning from the stables, she hadn't intended to change course. Having spent more time checking on her father's beloved horses than she should, she was already running behind schedule. But Perth with a knife was not something that she could ignore, and even though she knew it was most likely a mistake, she had veered to the left instead of continuing straight.

A good thing, as it turned out. What might he have

done to darling Sir Kensington had she not intervened? It wasn't the rooster's fault that he was loud. Nor was he to be blamed for the cracked corn that she had sprinkled under Perth's window.

After how flustered the duke had made her at dinner, she'd hoped to return the favor in kind. Between ending whist in the parlor and meeting her sisters in the Crescent Room, she had snuck outside to do the deed. Inhospitable of her, to say the least. But it was no less than what Perth deserved. Besides, what harm could come from rising with the sun? She'd never dreamt that he would wake up and go after Sir Kensington with a *butcher's knife*!

Now she was late to meet Richard, and flustered again besides. Her cousin was going to have questions. Questions that she needed to be able to answer calmly and assertively if she wanted to avoid his suspicion. If he thought for one *minute* that James was possibly dead, he'd have his solicitor knocking at the door with an army of servants behind him ready to move the sisters out and Richard in.

Not that it'd be quite as easy as that to remove them from their home. The courts would have to get involved. It would take weeks, if not months, before Richard was awarded the earldom and the all the property that went along with it. But wouldn't that be even worse? To know their fate (with no will to establish a legitimate claim, there wasn't a judge alive that would rule in favor of four women over a man) and be unable to change it.

Lenora could think of nothing worse.

Well, maybe one thing worse.

Make that one person.

But she wasn't able to dwell on *him* at the present moment. Not with Richard descending from his carriage in a swirl of rich purple silk and the pungent odor of cardamom; his favorite cologne.

He wore bright, royal bright colors to distract from his paleness. Paleness that often made it difficult to discern where his white blonde hair ended and his forehead began; a result of spending most of his childhood indoors.

Whenever Lenora and her sisters had paid him a visit, they'd often tried to draw him out into the sunshine to romp through the fields, but he had remained resolute in his decision to remain in the house playing jacks or terrorizing the family cat or yanking the wings off whatever poor insect made the mistake of getting trapped on the wrong side of the window.

Sickly. That was how his overly doting mother had described her only child as he was growing up.

*"Richard cannot go out in the rain, he is too sickly."*

*"Richard cannot go riding today, he is too sickly."*

*"Richard cannot travel for holiday, he is too sickly."*

Personally, Lenora had never witnessed any physical ailment aside from overall weakness courtesy of a sedentary lifestyle. But she didn't disagree with her aunt's assessment. Richard *was* sickly.

Just not in his body.

"Cousin," she greeted, pinning on her most welcoming smile as she ushered him inside. "I am so glad that you are here. How was your journey?"

"Awful." His voice, a pitch too high and nasally, as if his vocal chords resided somewhere inside of his nose instead of his throat, caused her smile to tighten at the edges. "The roads were terrible, the carriage was sweltering, and the food at the inn was horrendous."

"You came from London, then?" She stepped out of the way of several footmen as they carried Richard's numerous trunks through the foyer and up the stairs. There was enough luggage, she noted uneasily, for a six-month stay. Her gaze snapped back to her cousin. "I wasn't aware you were in the city."

"Last minute trip," he said with a careless wave of his arm before he stripped out of his traveling jacket and threw it at a passing maid. Removing his hat and tossing it to another maid, he smoothed a hand through the lacquered strands of his hair. "I needed to meet with my solicitor in person."

"Oh?" Lenora inquired pleasantly even as the nape of her neck went cold. "I do hope nothing is amiss."

"Just making some preparations," Richard said vaguely. "You know the kind."

No, she did *not* know the kind. But that was the point, wasn't it? To keep her guessing. To keep her and her sisters on their toes. Doubting. Questioning. Waiting for their odious cousin to make his move.

107

"And you mother? She is well?" They entered the front parlor. It was bustling with activity, most of the guests having risen and come downstairs to sate their hunger while Lenora was saving Sir Kensington's life.

Overall, everyone appeared a tad tired but happy as they gathered at the round tables the servants had set with antique lace cloths and a mix of sunflowers bursting from porcelain vases that matched the serving dishes. The windows were partially open, allowing a warm breeze to carry in the faint scent of honeysuckle. In the corner of the room Bridget played one of her original compositions on the pianoforte, her fingers flying effortlessly across the ivory keys. Annabel was already seated in between Lord and Lady Pratt, while Eloise piled a plate high with fruit, bread, and eggs. She turned and caught Lenora's gaze, who indicated with a subtle nod of her chin that Eloise ought to come over and say hello to Richard.

*'Coward'* she mouthed when her sister froze, then ducked behind the towering frame of Laird Glencairn and followed him and his bride to the furthest possible table, leaving Lenora to deal with their cousin on her own.

"Mother is fine," Richard answered as he browsed the sideboard and used silver tongs to select a strawberry. "She sends her best, and her apologies for not being here. The doctor has advised against travel due to her gout."

"I am sorry to hear that."

"Have you received any word from James on when he might bless us with his return?" A spoonful of sliced kiwi followed the lone strawberry on Richard's plate. He peered at her over his shoulder as he moved on to a vat of steaming porridge. His eyes were flat and glassy, like a trout's.

*No, not a trout,* Lenora thought.

A shark that had scented blood in the water and was beginning to circle.

"A letter came just last week," she lied. "He is sad to be missing the house party, but enjoying his extended holiday in Calcutta."

"Calcutta," Richard mused. He bit into the strawberry. A line of red juice started to dribble down the corner of his chin before he caught it with a linen napkin. "Home of the East India Company. Our James must be having a *very* lucrative trip."

Lenora frowned at the barbed insinuation. It was an open kept secret that one of the reasons the East India Company had taken a foothold in Calcutta was to deal in the opium trade. British smugglers were making a small fortune by bringing the addictive substance into China, where it was banned. The punishment for being caught was death, but that hadn't deterred the smugglers. There was too much coin to be made, and with the discreet backing of the British government they'd consistently grown more brazen, even going so far as to instigate a war with the Qing Dynasty under the guise of defending free trade.

It was a delicate situation. Supported by some,

abhorred by others. The East India Company had its roots in slavery, and while it had undoubtedly helped the British Empire expand its reach across the globe, the means by which the company had done so were inexcusable to many, including Lenora's parents. Her father had spoken openly against the powerful private conglomerate on the floor of Parliament. He'd even belonged to a committee formed with the specific purpose of abolishing it.

As far as she knew, James had always supported their father's political leanings. Or so she'd believed. But Richard's statement sowed a prickling line of doubt. What if he somehow *had* gotten involved with the opium trade during his travels in India? It might explain his disappearance and lack of communication.

Immediately, her mind flashed through the worst possible case scenarios. James, killed by a smuggler. Or starving to death in some horrible prison in Beijing. Or trapped in some opium den, a victim of his own addiction. Or some other end that was so terrible she was incapable of fathoming it.

She loved her brother.

Of all her siblings, he was the one she was closest too.

Probably since it had been just the two of them before Bridget, Annabel, and Eloise arrived.

But if he'd committed atrocious acts while on his Grand Tour–

No.

She wouldn't let herself even think it.

*If* James had become tangled up in smuggling, then it was because he was trying to stop it. The brother she knew, the brother she admired, the brother she adored, would never profit off the misery of others.

No matter what Richard implied.

"James has a friend who lives there." She took a plate as well, but didn't put any food on it. "Per his last letter, they are enjoying reminiscing about their time at Eton."

"Might I read the letter if you still have it?" Richard asked. "I miss my cousin. Seeing his handwriting would be a comfort."

*Oh, what a tangled web we weave, when first we practice to deceive!*

The line from Sir William Scot's famous poem, "Marmion: A Tale of Flodden Field", flitted through Lenora's head as her hands contracted around the plate she was holding with such force she wouldn't have been surprised if it cracked in half.

"Of course," she said with remarkable poise given the thunderous beat of her heart. "I'll see that it is delivered to your room. Now if you'll be so kind as to excuse me, I must have a quick word with the housekeeper. We're running low on oat cakes."

Without giving Richard the opportunity to respond, she bolted out of the parlor.

FROM A TABLE ACROSS the room, Perth sipped his coffee as he watched Lenora speak with a thin, blond-haired bloke that appeared vaguely familiar, although he couldn't quite place the skeletal frame and beady, lifeless black eyes with a name.

Whoever the man was, Lenora despised him.

Even more than she hated Perth, which was...interesting.

She was putting on a good front. Her smile was there, and she was making a grand show of actively listening to whatever Lord Bones was saying. But her shoulders were tense. And her face was a shade too pale.

No one else seemed to notice. But he did. Maybe because he'd been noticing everything about Lenora as of late.

The way that her hair glinted like onyx in the sunlight. The tiny wrinkle that showed itself in the middle of her nose whenever she was vexed, but also trying not to laugh. How easy it was to make her blush. And how rewarding it felt to watch those high cheekbones pinken with embarrassment.

Rewarding...and inexplicably arousing.

How far, he wondered, could that blush travel? If he said something truly outrageous, would it go all the way to her breasts? Changing the soft, white skin into a splendorous sunset of warm, rosy colors crowned with dusky–

No.

No, no.

He was supposed to be getting Lenora out of his head, not placing her directly onto his cock.

And that line of thought wasn't helpful at all, was it?

Blast and damn.

This was going to be harder than he'd anticipated.

In more ways than one.

"Who is that?" he asked Graham abruptly. The viscount was sitting next to him, reading a newspaper.

"To whom are you referring?" Graham replied without lifting his head.

"That bony chap over there by the sideboard. Speaking with Lady Lenora."

Graham folded the page and peered over the top of it. "Mr. Richard Rosewood. He was a year behind us at Eton."

Perth's brow creased. "Whiny prat that was always running to the headmaster with a case of the sniffles?"

"That's him."

"Don't people generally improve in appearance as they grow older?"

Graham lifted his shoulder in a noncommittal shrug.

Perth drummed his fingers on the table. He was unable to pinpoint precisely why, but there was something about

Richard Rosewood that bothered him. Immensely. "Why is he so thoroughly engaged with our hostess?"

"Richard's father and the late Earl of Clarenmore were brothers." Graham flipped to a new page. "He and Lady Lenora are cousins."

That explained their connection, then.

But not Lenora's underlying tension.

She wasn't filling her plate, he noted with a frown. Nor had she done much more at dinner the night before than nudge her food around with her fork. She needed to eat. She was already slender enough. Any more weight lost and the cheeks that he so enjoyed turning pink would begin to hollow.

"You're staring," Graham remarked mildly.

"The devil I am," Perth scowled even as he continued to stare.

The viscount sighed and laid his paper flat. "Weren't you telling me yesterday in the garden that I'd be best served to avoid Lady Lenora in my search for a wife? Now you're leering after her like some sort of besotted musk ox that's just spotted its mate." He lowered his voice. "She cannot be another one of your conquests."

"I'm not looking for a *conquest*." On a grumble of annoyance, Perth tore his gaze away from Lenora. "I'm not Attila the Hun. Or a bloody musk ox. That was rude."

"Then what are you looking for?" Graham's calm green eyes were too perceptive by far as he studied Perth's face. "Because I can almost assure you that Lady

114

Lenora Rosewood isn't it."

"And how would you know that? I'm a duke. She's a lady. Maybe we're perfectly suited for each other."

"You're not."

"No, we're not," Perth agreed. But damned if he wasn't tempted to...to do what, exactly? Court her? Bring her flowers and get down on bended knee and recite poetry? Because that's what a woman of Lenora's stature would expect. At a bare minimum. And he'd rather choke on his own tongue than memorize a line of Byron or Keats. "I think I need to see my doctor in London." His brow furrowed as he sipped his coffee. "I'm clearly not well."

"What about the youngest sister?" Graham suggested. "The redheaded one."

"Who?" Perth had yet to pay attention to any of the other Rosewoods. His sole focus had been, and continued to be, on Lenora. She was the sister that made his blood heat. The one that made him want to yank out his hair right before he yanked her against him.

"Lady Eloise. Or Lady Annabel. I don't know them personally, but it's obvious that either would be a better match than Lady Lenora if you're intent on finding a bride while you're here."

"Watch what you say," Perth growled. "I'm not finding a bride here or anywhere else. Are you trying to *curse* me?"

"No, but I am trying to prevent you from miring this

family in scandal."

"Since when do you suddenly care about the Rosewoods?"

Graham picked up his paper. "Since I decided that I am going to marry Lady Bridget."

"That was fast." Damned fast. Uncomfortably fast, when Perth considered that less than twenty-four hours ago neither he nor Graham had any wifely prospects in mind. Now Graham was engaged, and he was unable to stop himself from fantasizing about a prickly brunette. He didn't like the way this was going. He didn't like it at all. "Which one is she again?"

"The quiet blonde playing the pianoforte."

Curious, Perth stood halfway out of his chair to catch a glimpse of Graham's intended. He nodded approvingly. Shy, bookish chits weren't to his personal tastes, but he saw why Graham would like her. They could sit on opposite ends of their bed every night and read to their heart's content. "Congratulations."

"I have not officially proposed yet."

"How do you know that she'll yes, then?"

The viscount frowned. "Because it is logical that she do so."

*That* deserved a witty retort, but before Perth could think of one he saw Lenora rush out of the room. "I have to go," he said, nearly knocking over his coffee in his haste to stand.

"Monmouth," Graham began in a warning tone.

"What?"

"Be mindful of your step."

IF RICHARD WANTED to see a letter, then Lenora would show him a letter. One penned in her own hand, but if her cousin wasn't familiar with her brother's writing–and she had no reason to believe that he was–then he'd have no way of detecting her deception.

She'd just need to do it quickly, before everyone gathered to walk out to the southern field where a local falconer was going to put on a showy display with a pair of red-tailed hawks.

She was almost to her chamber, and the beautiful rosewood writing desk that had once belonged to her mother, when she heard the creak of a floorboard behind her. Stopping in the middle of the hallway, she turned and confronted none other than the Duke of Monmouth. Her constant shadow, or so it seemed these two days past.

"What?" she said incredulously. "What could you *possibly* want?"

He leaned a shoulder against the wall, the very picture of a disreputable rake with his hair spilling across his temple in a careless wave of gold and his hands shoved in the pockets of his trousers. "Would you believe me if I said I was just searching for the water closet?"

"No."

"What if I said I knew you were upset and I wanted to check on you?"

She pointed behind him. "There is a water closet through the first door on the left at the top of the stairs."

"That man you were talking to. Your cousin." While Perth's mouth was curved in a lazy grin, his brown eyes were sharp and assessing. "Why don't you like him?"

"Who said I did not like him?" Outside of the immediate family, nobody was aware of the strain that existed between the Rosewood sisters and Richard. Even *they* hardly acknowledged it. How, then, had Perth sensed the truth? That she not only didn't like Richard, she *loathed* him. That he was not here by her consent, but his own will. That his very presence was a threat.

"You did. Your body language." Perth shifted, casting half of his frame into shadow while the rest remained in the light. An apt setting for a man with the face of an angel and the heart of a devil. "The way you held your chin. The set of your spine. The flex of your fingers as they wrapped around the plate that you never put any food on."

"I wasn't…" Her tongue skimmed between her lips. "I wasn't aware that you had nothing better to do with your time than stare at other people."

"Not other people." A husky note entered his voice; velvet being dragged along a rough patch of cobblestone. "Only you, Lenora."

*Only you, Lenora.*

The words slipped beneath her skin like quicksilver, causing her blood to tingle as it rushed through her veins. Were she in love with Perth, they'd be words that she longed to hear. That she yearned to hear.

But she wasn't.

And they weren't.

"*Lady* Lenora," she corrected firmly. That distinction–that buffer of propriety–was important to maintain. Essential, really. Without it, they were just a woman and a man, alone in a hallway, with no one around…and nothing to stop their most carnal imaginings from becoming reality.

The corner of Perth's mouth quirked. "Lady Lenora," he repeated, but he spoke her name in such a soft, intimate way–as if it were a whisper between lovers–that it was almost worse.

"You–you cannot be here, with me." Her hands curled into fists, nails anchoring themselves into her palms through the thin layer of her wrist-length kid gloves. "You need to leave."

"What do you think is going to happen? Do you think I am going to kiss you? You do," he breathed when her face warmed. "What a high opinion you have of yourself, Lady Lenora."

"It's not a high opinion. It's fact." She tugged at her bodice. Was it hot in here? She needed to remind the maids to open the windows at the end of the hallway first

119

thing in the morning to let in the cool, damp air before the afternoon sun took hold. "Your reputation precedes you, Your Grace. It's well known that you'd kiss a chair if it was wearing a skirt. I don't regard myself as special. I'm simply a female in a dress."

"Yes, you are." His eyes took on a dark gleam as he stepped away from the wall. The thick runner swallowed up the sound of his footsteps so that he walked to her in silence. Not that she'd have been able to hear him above the pounding of her own pulse. He reached out and brushed a curl behind her ear, his knuckles glancing across her cheek in a soft caress that made her knees tremble. "It's a very pretty dress."

"What–what are you doing?" she said warily.

Perth groaned. "The hell if I know."

Then he clasped her face with his hands and took her mouth with his own.

# 9

## *Duke Got Your Tongue?*

THE KISS SHOULD not have taken Lenora by surprise, but it did. Or if not the act itself, then her reaction to it. Which wasn't to shove Perth away, as she *should* have done. But rather to grab onto the lapels of his jacket in order to steady herself as she met his passion with her own long suppressed desires.

It wasn't until she'd been tempted with wickedness that part of her realized how exhausting it was to be good all the time. To mind her manners, and keep her sisters in line, and maintain an orderly household. To be everything for everyone, all the while pushing her own needs and her own wants down deeper, and deeper, until they simply…disappeared. Only to be resurrected by the Duke of Monmouth, of all people. A dissolute rogue whom she had *no* business kissing in the hallway. Or anywhere else, for that matter. Yet here she stood, doing just that.

And it was *wonderful.*

Forbidden, and sensuous, and tantalizing delightful. Like when she'd snuck downstairs and eaten an entire chocolate cake by herself. She had paid for it later with a terrible bellyache. There were always consequences for the crimes of the impulsive. But oh, that first decadent mouthful of rich, silky chocolate slowly melting on her tongue had been worth every moment of discomfort that came after.

And so was this.

A mewling whimper escaped from her lips when he boldly slid his tongue inside to lick, and taste, and touch what no man had ever dared. Perth's kiss was unapologetically bold. It wasn't a question, but a statement. Not a query, but a claiming. Of *her*.

If she'd thought the hallway warm before, it was positively scorching now.

On a feral growl that ignited licks of flame between her thighs, he backed her up against the wall. A portrait of her great-great-grandmother rattled in its frame when he captured her wrists in his hand and yanked them above her head, exposing her to the sheer strength of his lust. It would have been intimidating, if not for the answering quiver of excitement that pulsed low in her belly.

She wanted this.

There was a part of her that desperately *needed* this.

To relinquish control. To revel in her own vulnerability. To be dominated by a force more powerful than herself.

And oh, what a force Perth was.

He commanded her as if she were a pianoforte and he a pianist. Directing her body to play whatever melody those long, nimble fingers and hot mouth desired.

A snarl tore itself loose from the depths of his throat, and moisture beaded between her thighs in response to the feral sound. Angling his head, he deepened the kiss as his fingers dove into her hair, scattering pins in every direction. His teeth caught on her bottom lip, delivering a sharp nip that elicited a soft gasp. A gasp that turned into a moan when he soothed the bite with his tongue.

The hand holding her wrists pinned helplessly against the wall tightened, then released to cup her breast, thumb gliding across her nipple. Blood rushed to the tip, hardening it into an aching nub of pure sensation. Fire kindled anew in her belly when he yanked her bodice down, and her breast spilled out, and he drew her nipple into the searing confines of his mouth.

In Lenora's opinion, her bosom had always been one of the least favorite parts of her anatomy. She knew the basic mechanism her breasts provided, but without a child to nurse, to her they were useless, awkward things that got in the way more often than not.

Now, however…*now* she understood their appeal.

She'd just needed a fair haired devil to show it to her.

"Do you like when I kiss you there?" Perth's eyes glittered like stars in a midnight sky as he raised his chin and took hold of her gaze. A lazy smile claimed his lips, but his jaw was clenched, hinting at dark, turbulent waters under the sea of charming calm.

Her answer was a hesitant nod, causing his smile to widen.

"Naughty minx," he murmured huskily. "Where else should I kiss you?"

Where else? Did that mean there places *other* than her mouth and breasts that his wicked mouth could claim as his own? Both scandalized and intrigued by the idea, she racked her brain for a proper response.

"My–my neck?" she ventured.

"Oh, Lady Lenora." His raspy chuckle brought a flush to her cheeks. "I think we can do better than *that*."

There was a bench further down the hall. He took her by the hand and led her to it as if she were a docile lamb and he a wolf leading her off into the woods to be devoured. She didn't resist when he put pressure on her shoulders and pushed her into a sitting position. Her bones had abandoned her, she was only heat and blood and short, pulsing breaths.

Dimly she was aware of the fact that at any second, a servant might come tromping up the stairs and discover them. Or even worse, a sister. But instead of diminishing her pleasure, the risk of being found merely served to enhance it.

"What are you doing?" she asked when he knelt between her legs and nudged her trembling thighs apart.

"Finding other places to kiss you. Hold this."

While she gaped at the top of his head, he gave her a handful of her own skirts, followed promptly by her chemise. She was wearing a corset but had forgone her crinoline; it was too heavy and cumbersome for a walk out to the southern field. Which meant only a single article of clothing remained to shield the most intimate part of her body from Perth's lascivious advance. Her cotton drawers, tied at the waist and at the juncture of her thighs with a slip of silk ribbon that was no match for the duke's fingers.

"What–what are you *doing?*" she repeated shrilly. "You cannot possibly find anything to kiss down *there*."

"On the contrary," he said, his voice muffled as his mouth began a burning ascent up her calf, dressed in a silk stocking, to her knee, to her thigh, to her–

Oh God.

Oh God.

"Oh *God,*" she cried when she felt his mouth, warm and wet.

His tongue followed the damp seam in the middle of her curls to the small, innocent pearl of flesh that she'd never given much consideration to. When he gently suckled the room spun, sunlight swirling into shadow and shadow into sunlight as she grasped his hair and held on for dear life. To her absolute mortification her hips bucked off the bench, and he took the opportunity to slide his hands beneath her buttocks, each palm squeezing a cheek while he continued to torment her in the most delicious, decadent way possible.

In this scenario, *she* was the rich chocolate cake.

And he was lapping her up one crumb at a time.

"Sweet," he said hoarsely. "You taste so bloody sweet."

A good thing his face was in her thighs, as he couldn't see *her* face turn as red as a ripe tomato.

She started to stiffen. To pull away. To retreat behind that familiar steel curtain of decorum. What was Perth doing? What was *she* doing? Sprawled on the bench in the hallway with her legs splayed over a duke's shoulders?

A sin.

She was committing an egregious sin.

*That's* what she was doing.

But if this was what it was like to be a sinner...then she never wanted to be a saint.

A sense of urgency began to stir within her. As if she were climbing towards some peak hiding in the clouds. Her legs quivered, the long muscles contracting as the heels of her shoes dug into Perth's back and her fingers knotted in his hair, brazenly holding him to her.

The hands cupping her bottom tightened, he tilted her hips, and then his tongue was inside her. As it had been inside of her mouth. But there must have been more nerve endings down *there*, for she came off the bench with a desperate cry as wave after wave crashed over her.

When it was over, when it was done, she slid limply off the bench to sit on the floor beside Perth in a pool of satin and silk. Vaguely, she noted that his arm was looped behind her waist, his fingers idly stroking up and down her arm. His visage was turned in the other direction, providing her with the barest glimpse of his profile. Those thick brows, capable of so much sarcasm. His nose, straight and noble. That remarkable jawline. And his mouth...lips shiny from tasting her.

As embarrassment sliced through her hazy wave of euphoria and the gravity of her actions settled squarely on her shoulders, Lenora lurched forward out of his embrace and scrambled clumsily to her feet.

"You...I...we..."

Perth drew up his knee and rested his elbow on it. As casual as if they'd just had tea in the drawing room. "I believe the words you're searching for are 'thank you'," he drawled, arching one of those sardonic brows.

Her face paled, then flooded with color. "You are–you are–"

"Duke got your tongue?" A second brow rose to join the first. "Or should I say, your quim."

*Death*, Lenora thought.

Surely death would be preferable to having to stand here and endure Perth's insufferable arrogance. Grinding her teeth together, she began to look for her hairpins. She'd need to return her coiffure to some semblance of normalcy before she went downstairs and forgot that any of this had ever happened. But when she tried to retrieve a pin from beside the duke, he closed his fingers around her wrist.

"I can all but see the wheels in that clever brain of yours spinning round," he said quietly. "What are you thinking, Lenora?"

She didn't bother to correct him this time.

They were far, *far* past any governing rules of propriety.

"You know what I am thinking." Yanking free of his grasp, she retrieved her pin and withdrew to a safe distance to fix her curls. No easy task, given the sheer mass of her hair. Unbound, it nearly reached her waist. But she'd just have to do her best as the alternative–ringing for Bree–was out of the question. No one, not even her lady's maid who was privy to more intimate details of her life than even her siblings, could know about her temporary lapse in judgment. "This never should have happened." In her agitated state she jabbed too hard with a pin and hissed in pain when it bounced off her scalp. "As far as I am concerned, it did *not* happen."

"Here." Perth stood and motioned for her to turn. "Let me."

"What do you know about styling hair?" she asked

128

bitingly.

"Clearly more than you." His mahogany gaze held its usual glint of mocking amusement, but there was another emotion there as well. Something that she couldn't quite decipher. That she wasn't sure if she *wanted* to decipher.

"Fine." She slapped the pins into his hand, then spun on her heel and held her breath as she felt him begin to gather the long, inky tendrils. Since she was a girl, her hair had been combed and brushed and fixed into a braid, or a bun, or an elaborate coiffure nearly every day of her life. Rarely had she done it herself, relying instead on the far more talented skills of a servant. Occasionally her mother. Maybe Annabel. But never a man.

Perth's breath was warm and steady against her nape. His hands inexplicably gentle as he twisted and pinned her curls into place. In a strange way, it was almost more intimate than the kisses they'd shared.

"I suppose you've done this for hundreds of women," she said, the statement as much for herself as it was for him. A not-so-subtle reminder that Perth was a rogue, and a hellion, and if she permitted herself to develop any sort of tender for him then *she* was an idiot.

"Hundreds?" His short whistle stirred the tiny wisps of hair behind her ear that were too short to be caught up in pins. "I'm flattered. Truly. But you're the first."

"As if I am to believe that," she scoffed even as her heart gave a small, silly flutter.

"Believe what you'd like. All done." He rubbed his

hands together as he moved aside and gestured for her to check the results in a nearby mirror.

After casting him a suspicious glare over her shoulder, she went to the silvery glass half-expecting to see a frizzled bird's nest lumped on top of her head. Instead, she found a perfectly presentable coiffure with nary a strand out of place.

Perth met her stunned gaze in the mirror and smirked. "What can I say? I'm a man of many talents."

"Scoundrel, more like," she muttered under her breath.

"How odd," he said blandly. "You weren't nearly this quarrelsome when I was licking your–"

"We are *not* discussing that." She spun around and pointed her finger at him. "It didn't happen."

He snorted. "It damned well did."

"No, it didn't."

"Then how do I know that when you're on the cusp of coming, you make a breathy little purring noise in the back of the throat?"

She had *purred?*

No, no she hadn't. Because the only way she was going to get through the rest of the house party was to pretend that this–this interlude in the hallway had never occurred. There was never any kissing. Or touching. And there was absolutely *no* purring.

"I am not responsible for your lurid imagination, Your Grace." Her bodice was askew. Sucking in her ribcage, she adjusted the boning of her corset, then gave her skirts a shake for good measure. There. Everything was as it had been. As if Perth had never come sauntering up those stairs and backed her up against the wall and–

"You're blushing again," he observed.

"I'm not," she said stubbornly.

His eyes rolled. "You can lie to me all you want. But you cannot lie to yourself."

"I am not lying. I am *choosing* to forget the last ten minutes ever happened." Her chin lifted a notch. "There is a difference."

"Why would you want to forget?" he said, sounding genuinely perplexed. "The giving and receiving of pleasure is nothing to be ashamed of. *I'm* certainly not going to forget what we did."

That gave her pause. "You're not?"

"No. Because it was bloody brilliant." He bowed his forehead to hers. His skin was remarkably cool, while her temple still felt hot and slightly sticky from the thin sheen of perspiration that had covered it during the height of their passion. "*You're* brilliant, minx. All that heat and fire contained in an icy prison of your own making. But we managed to melt down a bar. Maybe even two. Don't be so quick to put them back up."

"I…" She wet her lips. "I don't know what you're talking about."

It was dizzying, to be this close to him. In her studies, she'd read that the sun exerted a large amount of gravitational pull due to its sheer size in relation to the earth. Scientists and astronomers were continuing to research the effects of the massive star on their planet, but one thing was certain: if the earth ever got too close, it would be incinerated. In that way, Perth and the sun were similar. He was dazzlingly bright and far more beautiful than any man had a right to be. But with that beauty and that brightness came the danger of being burned.

Perth was a duke, but she stood firm in her belief that he was *not* a suitable candidate for a husband. Nor was she about to lower herself by becoming his mistress. That left them with the in-between. With this. Stolen moments of lust in hallways and broom closets. Hoping they weren't discovered even as that risk spurred on the flames of their desire.

Maybe if her situation were different…maybe if she wasn't responsible for her sisters, and protecting her brother's title, and honoring her parent's memory…maybe if she wasn't constantly burdened by the weight of her own expectations…maybe then…

But those were already too many maybes.

And she would rather stay safe in her prison of ice than step outside and be blinded by the sun.

"I need…I need to fetch something from my bedchamber."

"Lenora—"

"And you need to return downstairs." She didn't have the will to fight him. Not now. Not until she found her proverbial footing again. "*Please*, Your Grace."

He searched her gaze. Whatever he saw there caused his eyes to narrow, his pupils twin spots of black trapped within intense circles of burnt sienna. He started to speak. Stopped. Without another word, he walked away.

# 10

### *Scots and Hawks*

DAMN WOMEN, Perth thought furiously as he fell in line with the rest of the guests making their way outside for some ridiculous hawk demonstration.

Wait.

He didn't mean that.

By and large, women were glorious, magnificent creatures. Compassionate, giving, and selfless, they'd had his appreciation from an early age. He might have despised his sire, but he'd always held his mother in high regard. As he did his past paramours, and mistresses, and the spellbinding circus performer that had ridden into the tent on an elephant...and later ridden him to sweet ecstasy in much the same fashion.

No, women were just splendid. Particularly given the shite they had to deal with courtesy of men.

Damn wo*man*.

There.

That was better.

His ire was strictly reserved for one female in particular.

Unfortunately, she was also the only female he wanted to fuck.

"What's crawled up yer arse and died?" Laird Glencairn asked cheerfully as he came abreast of Perth and gave him a friendly poke in the ribs with his elbow.

"Excuse me?" Perth responded coolly.

While other recipients of the Duke of Monmouth's wrath would have immediately found a rock to hide under, the brash Scotsman just grinned. "Ye look like ye've been sucking on a lemon. Canna be the weather, as the sky's blue as Loch Lomond in August. Word has it ye are rich as the dickens, so it canna be that either. And far as I can tell, ye are in good health, so it's not a case of the gout."

"I do not have *gout*," Perth snapped, mildly offended.

"Aye, that's what I jest said." Glencairn walked around a cluster of shrubbery and rejoined him on the other side. "Which means either ye are a miserable bastard in general, or ye are suffering from lady troubles."

Inadvertently, Perth's gaze shot ahead to the front of

the wandering line where Lenora, her face obscured by a massive straw hat, led the way up a small, grassy embankment along with two of her sisters.

"Lady troubles," Glencairn said with great satisfaction. "Suspected as much."

"Do you even know who I am?" Perth wondered aloud.

"Aye, the Duke of Monmouth."

"Very good. Then you must also know that I don't have *lady* troubles."

The massive Scotsman gave him a hearty slap on the back that nearly sent him careening into a nearby tree. "We all have lady troubles, *charaid*."

Perth straightened his coat. Where the devil was Graham? The viscount was as bland as an old sock, but at least he refrained from unruly gestures of affection.

"Aren't you a newlywed?" he asked. "Surely your bride cannot detest you already."

"Aye, I am. That's my bonny lass there." Glencairn pointed proudly at a slim, red-haired woman several yards ahead walking dutifully alongside Lady Greer. "I've loved her since I was a lad. Took a bit of convincing on her part. But she came around eventually. That's not tae say we don't have our problems now and again. She's feisty, me Brenna. And I'm stubborn. A hardy combination, tae be sure. But when yer heart finds the one it's meant tae reside with, then the troubles are worth it."

"And *why* are you telling me this?" Perth wasn't rude by nature. All right, yes he was. But generally that rudeness was tempered with a heavy dose of sarcastic wit, the better to fool whomever he was talking to into thinking that he gave a damn about their opinion. But the Scot's words had struck a touch too close to home, leaving an uncomfortable, chalky taste in the back of his throat.

His heart?

*Reside* with someone?

Again, his gaze went to Lenora. The taste of chalk intensified. After a cursory glance around to make sure no one was looking at him, he turned his head and spat on the ground.

To hell with hearts and lady troubles.

To hell with nosy Scots, too.

There was a reason their two countries had such a tumultuous history.

The brawny bastards couldn't take a hint to save their lives.

"I'm telling ye this tae lighten yer step, *charaid*, and ease that scowl before it sticks." The corners of Glencairn's eyes crinkled with humor as he grinned. He started to lift his hand for another friendly slap on the shoulder, then wisely lowered it when he saw Perth's hostile expression.

A snarling, rapid dog was positively loving when compared to the Duke of Monmouth in the midst of a foul mood. Glencairn *could* have touched him again, but chances were high that he'd come away with a few less fingers than what he'd started with.

"No harm intended," the Scotsman said lightly. "Just trying tae save ye the hardship that I went through."

"When I require advice, I'll ask for it." Perth paused. "Congratulations on your nuptials."

The path opened up into a wide field of rippling ryegrass and daisies. A man stood in the middle beneath a clear expanse of blue, his outstretched arm the roost for a large bird with sharp talons and a curved beak that would have given Sir Kensington a run for his money. Its head was covered in a round leather hood, and upon seeing the way that it was contained, Perth experienced a twinge of pity for the poor beast. A hawk was supposed to be free. To soar, and hunt, and kill. Not be tied to the limb of some bloody human with a blindfold over its eyes.

While the other guests *oohed* and *aahed* and clustered together for a closer look, he fell back to observe from a distance. But as the hawk was released to soar high above their heads, his mind wasn't with the bird of prey in the sky but rather with the raven-haired beauty on the ground.

His raw, magnetic attraction to Lenora puzzled him. He hadn't wanted to kiss her in the hallway. He'd *needed* to. As much as he'd needed to take his next breath. And while attraction and women went hand in hand, usually so too did his self-control.

He was careful, exquisitely so, not to sip from the same pools that he swam in. As a duke, his presence was required at balls, and house parties, and soirees. But the type of ladies who frequented such events–ladies like Lenora Rosewood–were far too pure for the likes of him. Which was why, traditionally, he gave them a wide berth.

A dance, a dinner, a devilish look now and again...but never a kiss.

Until Lenora.

He removed his glove and scratched his chin, then absently ran his thumb across his bottom lip. A lip that still held the faintest taste of Lenora.

God, but she'd been sweet.

Honey, and sugar, and a hint of tangy citrus.

He could have eaten her all day, and into the night.

When her slick muscles had contracted around his tongue...

Heaven.

He could have sworn he'd seen heaven.

Or if not the pearly gates themselves, then surely an angel. An angel with heavy lidded blue eyes and smooth satin skin and a tumbling waterfall of ebony hair that had twined around his arms like a veil as he'd pleasured her.

The small whimpering cries that she'd made as she drew closer and closer to orgasm...when the moon was up, and his hand was around his cock, he would need only the memory of those sounds to bring himself to release.

And that was a problem.

A bloody big problem.

Enormous, really (all his mistresses said so).

Wasn't it just this morning that he'd told himself he wouldn't kiss her? Because kissing would inevitably lead to fucking, and fucking to marriage. But it was hardly past noon, and he'd already had his head under Lenora's skirts and his tongue in her tight little quim.

So much for best intentions.

At least he *hadn't* fucked her.

Not in a way that might have consequences in nine months' time. Or force him into a marriage that he didn't want, as he wasn't such a scoundrel that he would take a lady's innocence and then not bother to make an honest woman of her.

But he'd come close.

Damned close.

Had anyone walked up those stairs, he'd have had to propose on the spot, or else condemn Lenora to a life of ruin.

Just the thought of seeing those proud shoulders bent in shame twisted his gut. He would not be the reason for her ostracism from the *ton*. Lenora's fate was already written. In a week, a month, a year, she'd find a nice viscount, or an earl, or even a duke. He would court her appropriately. No head under her skirt, or hands on that deliciously plump arse. Just a peck on the cheek and maybe a bit of hand holding sans gloves, if the fellow got lucky. At the end of the Season they'd become betrothed, and then married. She would have a son with her blue eyes and a daughter with her black hair. Then she'd spend the rest of her life presiding over a manor in Grosvenor Square and an estate in Sussex. There'd be house parties galore.

And Perth wouldn't take that from her.

Not when he had no alternative to offer.

Lenora wasn't made to be a mistress, and he wasn't about to make himself a husband. Thus whatever this mad, all-consuming desire to possess her was, it could proceed no further. He and Lenora were done. Over. Ended. Finished. Commenced.

This time, he really meant it.

And he *did* try.

Truly.

…until he didn't.

# 11

## *Ghosts*

RICHARD SUSPECTS SOMETHING is amiss," Annabel said flatly as she entered the Crescent Room. It was two days after the hawk demonstration, and they'd concluded the evening with yet another rousing game of whist in the drawing room. Lady Renalta, daughter of the Marquess and Marchioness of Donegal, had taken the last round and unseated the reigning champion, Lady Pratt, in a small victory for wallflowers everywhere.

Startled by Annabel's ominous declaration, Lenora set aside the embroidery she had been using to settle her mind, an old tactic that she'd learned at her mother's knee. While the past twelve hours had gone by largely without incident (aside from Laird Glencairn imbibing too much brandy at dinner and leading the entire room in a rousing rendition of "Love is a Lassie"), her nerves had been dancing on a wire since...well, since The Kiss That Was Forgotten.

Of course, her kiss with Perth *hadn't* been forgotten. Not even a little bit. Thus the needle and thread that was attached to her hand whenever all the guests went to bed and her duties as a hostess ended for the today. It was either embroidery, or she laid awake in bed staring at the ceiling, remembering, in vivid detail, the fiery brand of Perth's fingers on her body and the demanding pressure of his mouth on her lips and the teasing flick of his tongue between her legs...

The next morning, she'd had a footman remove the bench to another part of the house. If only she could remove her own memories so easily. But it seemed the harder that she tried to strike the Duke of Monmouth from her thoughts, the more pervasive he became.

He was *everywhere*.

Even when he was nowhere.

At breakfast she'd actually had to stop herself from looking for him. During Bridget's pianoforte recital in the music room she'd wondered why he wasn't there. And when he sat at the opposite end of the table at dinner, she'd experienced an unmistakable flicker of disappointment.

Perth was doing what she had asked of him.

He was leaving her alone.

Leaving *her* to commit self-inflicted torture.

Twenty more days, she reminded herself.

Twenty days, and the house party would be over.

Twenty days, and Perth would be out from under her roof.

Twenty days.

But the way her traitorous heart leapt whenever she saw him, it might as well have been twenty *years*.

"What makes you believe Richard is suspicious?" Deliberately placing Perth by the wayside, Lenora focused her full attention on Annabel. "He hasn't said anything to me."

Truth be told, their cousin hadn't spoken more than a few cordial words to her since she'd handed him the faux letter from James. Leaving her to assume, or at least hope, that her fears concerning any brewing plot to take control of the earldom and Clarenmore Park were largely unfounded.

"Or me," said Bridget from the chaise lounge where she was tucked cozily under a blanket with a book.

"Has Richard *ever* talked to you?" Annabel asked.

"No," Bridget replied after she thought it over for a moment. "I'm not even sure he knows that Mother and Father had a third daughter. Can I go back to reading? I have just gotten to the part where the hero is about to proclaim his love for the heroine."

"Why does he have to proclaim it?" Lenora frowned. "Why isn't it insinuated?"

"Because in the previous chapter he made a terrible

mistake, and now he has to grovel," Bridget said happily. "I *love* it when they grovel."

Lenora's frown deepened. "Why could he just not have done something that he'd need to grovel for? What sort of author would purposefully put their characters through such unnecessary angst?"

"A romantic one," her sister sighed.

"Nora's version of romance is a rousing garden party where the hero and heroine discuss the weather," Annabel snickered. "Later they take a long stroll past the china cabinet where she lectures him on the varying color patterns of blue and white porcelain."

"It is not," Lenora said defensively. "I simply don't understand why a couple cannot find satisfaction in common interests without miring themselves in turmoil. And what is so wrong about discussing the weather anyway? It is a perfectly fine topic of conversation."

"Perfectly *boring*, you mean," said Annabel.

"Why would anyone want to read a book about a hero and heroine who spend their time taking tours of the china cabinet?" Bridget asked, confused.

Lenora huffed. "That's not what–"

"When *I* fall in love," Annabel interrupted, "I want it be just like from one of your books, Bridge. My hero and I will have a heated argument, and then he is going to sweep me off my feet in a shower of rose petals after he professes his undying love. It shall be the ultimate act of devotion, and we'll ride off into the sunset on a white horse."

"That sounds wonderful," Bridget said dreamily.

"It *sounds* like a recipe for disaster." Lenora's hand twitched in agitation as she picked up a seam ripper and began to yank out a series of unwanted stitches from her embroidery pattern. "These–these ardent love affairs are all well and good on paper, but they'd hardly work in the real world. No amount of groveling can magically transform a ne'er-do-well into a paragon of virtue, and a heroine can only be expected to endure so many witty remarks! What if she has a family that needs tending?" *Rrriiiip.* The first stitch came loose. "Or sisters to be married off before she can dedicate herself to finding the right husband?" *Rrriiiip.* The second popped free. "Naturally, everyone wants the scoundrel who makes their knees wobble and their insides quiver! But such a man just isn't practical."

Annabel slanted Bridget a sideways glance. "Who said anything about quivering insides?" she whispered.

Bridget shrugged. "I don't know, but I'm going to pen a letter to Ms. Cleghorn. That should *definitely* be included in her next book."

"Furthermore," Lenora continued through gritted teeth as she worked the sharp edge of the seam ripper under an offending green thread, "what would the expected longevity of such a match be? The first few months would no doubt be a haze of euphoric bliss–"

*'Euphoric bliss?'* Annabel mouthed silently.

"–but what about after? When the love has worn off and the lust has faded, what then? A marriage of infidelity and loneliness, that's what. Because two people need more than emotions to sustain a marriage!" She slashed blindly at the remaining stitching. "A successful union requires sacrifice and shared hobbies and mutual respect. Not white horses and castles in the clouds and passionate embraces in hallways!"

"Have you read this book already?" Bridget flipped excitedly through the pages. "I haven't gotten to the hallway part yet."

Annabel, who was studying Lenora closely, said, "I don't think she was referring to your book."

Lenora's chest heaved as she gazed at the tattered remnants of her embroidery pattern. When tears blurred her vision, she blinked them angrily away. The control that she expected of herself– that she *demanded* of herself–was slipping away. And for that, she blamed Perth.

*He* had made her like this. Her head was in a perpetual fog because of him and his–his damned kisses! They were all she could think about, when she should have been concentrating on the house party. He'd robbed her of her common sense. Of her very sanity! For surely the only explanation for why her pulse quickened and her heart pitter-patted whenever he walked into the room was complete and utter lunacy. He'd driven her mad. That's what he'd done. With his smoldering stare and his arrogant smirks and his sensuous mouth.

Were it in her capabilities to do so, she would have banished him from Clarenmore Park on the spot. But she could no more be rid of a duke than she could order the sun not to rise.

*Twenty days.*

Twenty days, and she'd be rid of Perth.

On a deep breath, she pried the hoop loose from the handkerchief she'd ruined and reached for a fresh square of lawn linen.

"I am glad that you glean such enjoyment from your books, Bridget," she said pleasantly. "Reading is a wonderful escape, so long as one remembers that fictional characters are just that. Fictional. And hardly representative of the qualities one might seek in a real husband."

Bridget's pale brows drew together. "But I *do* want a husband that is handsome and dashing, and with whom I share a strong physical connection. A husband that is madly in love with me, and who I love in return."

"Yes, that all seems fine when it's written in a book," Lenora responded, and this time her voice held a definable clip of impatience. "But in reality, I am afraid that such a man would prove to be exceedingly troublesome and vexing. There are far more important things than appearance and attraction. Like moral strength of character, for instance."

Annabel's head canted slyly to the side. "What about

wealth and title?"

"Naturally, his social standing, and ability to provide a stable environment for his wife and any children they might have together, must be considered as well. While a title is no longer an essential requirement given the success of private businessmen, a lady of gentle breeding cannot be expected to sustain a comfortable living should she marry a pauper." She threaded her needle. "Which, might I add, is another reason to avoid following the impulses of one's heart and marrying strictly for handsomeness or physical connectivity. A marriage, a *successful* marriage that is beneficial to both parties, is as much a business transaction as it is anything else."

"But then what about, oh, I don't know..." Annabel tapped her chin as she wandered over to the window and peered out into the inky darkness. "A duke?"

"What about a duke?" Lenora said guardedly.

"That *would* be the ultimate prize, wouldn't it? Surely such a lofty title would compensate for a lack of moral character. And if he wasn't hideously ugly, and had all of his teeth, and wasn't old enough to be our grandfather, well, I should presume that would put him at the front of the list. From a business perspective, that is." She turned around. "Bridget, have you noticed if the Duke of Monmouth is in possession of all his teeth?"

Bridget blinked at the question. "I haven't examined his molars, but I am fairly certain that he does."

"This has *nothing* to do with the Duke of Monmouth."

Incensed, Lenora stabbed her needle through the linen with too much force. The sharp tip struck her finger on the other side, and when a spot of red stained the fabric she cursed aloud. "*Damnit!* Now look what you've made me do."

"Did you just swear?" Fresh from a bath, Eloise chose that inopportune moment to enter the room wrapped in an oversized dressing robe and dripping water in her wake. Her red hair was slicked back from her face and she wore a grin that stretched from one ear to the other, while above it her eyes sparkled with mirth. "I am marking this date in my journal."

"Lenora was just sharing with us all the reasons why we shouldn't marry for love," said Annabel.

"That's not what I–"

"Or physical attraction," Bridget piped in.

"I didn't mean–"

"Or euphoric bliss," Annabel added solemnly.

"What is left?" Eloise asked, perching on the armrest of Bridget's chair.

"Your sisters are being difficult, and having fun at my expense." Moving stiffly, Lenora returned her failed embroidery attempts to her sewing basket and rose to her feet. "It is neither kind, nor productive. I am heading to bed. *Someone* has to plan for the daily activities tomorrow."

"Nora, we're terribly sorry," Bridget exclaimed, tossing her book aside. "We didn't mean to hurt your feelings!"

"We didn't hurt her feelings." Annabel hands went to her hips as a golden brow arched. "We merely pointed out all the fallacies in her preposterous theory on marriage. And why she hasn't listed a single satisfactory reason for not pursuing a courtship with the Duke of Monmouth."

Lenora stopped in front of her door. "I have a *hundred* reasons."

"Name one," Annabel demanded.

"I…He…I…I don't owe you an explanation!" She glared at her sisters over her shoulder. "Any of you. I've made it clear that the Duke of Monmouth isn't a suitable match for a husband, and that's the end of it! I do not wish to discuss him, or this topic, any further."

"Just because he makes you uncomfortable does not mean that he's unsuitable," Annabel shot back. "You need someone who challenges you, Lenora. Or else you'll be bored to tears before your first anniversary."

"You like everything to be orderly and precise," said Eloise. "But that isn't life. That isn't love."

Bridget nodded in agreement. "Sophialynne, the heroine in my book, despises the hero at first. They're always at odds. Bickering about this and that." She started to giggle. "There was one scene, with a goose, where they–"

"Get on with it, Bridge," Annabel said.

Left unchecked, Bridget would have blissfully

summarized the book line by line.

She'd done it before.

Ad nauseam.

"Sorry." A sheepish smile claimed her lips. "All I am saying, is that sometimes the person you *least* expect to fall in love with is the one that you do. Just like Sophialynne and her Pendergast."

"Sophialynne and *Pendergast?*" Eloise said skeptically.

"What's wrong with that?" Bridget asked.

"Those are the most absurd names I've ever heard."

"I think they're romantic."

"You think *rocks* are romantic."

Bridget scooted to the far side of her chair and scowled at her sister. "The ones that couples carve their names into *are* romantic."

Eloise snorted. "Just what I want a suitor to do. Write my name on a rock. Although, if it kept him busy and away from me…"

Lenora wasn't listening to her siblings fight. The sound of it was so normal as to fade straight into the background. Her mind was on other matters. And her heart…her heart wasn't to be trusted at the moment.

"Our brother is missing," she cut in, and the squabbling immediately ceased. Her throat tightened, warning her not to say the words that stuck to the roof of her mouth like jam, but they needed to be spoken aloud. For all of them. Maybe then, this ridiculous notion that she and Perth were somehow meant to be because he infuriated her like no other would stop, and they could get on with their lives in an organized fashion.

"Our brother is missing," she repeated. "Maybe even dead. We are in the midst of a house party. Our cousin is undoubtedly conspiring against us to take our home. And on top of it all, we are preparing to relaunch ourselves into Society sans scandal. I haven't the *time* to fall in love. Even if I did, I can assure you that it would not be with the Duke of Monmouth."

"But–" Annabel began.

"That is the end of it. No more. *No more.*" Not wanting to give her sisters the chance to muster a rebuttal, she opened her door and retreated into her room. But even though she was already dressed for bed, and the day had been tiresome, and the hour was late, it was a long, long while before she managed to fall asleep.

IN A SEPARATE PART of the house, Perth was suffering through an equally unpleasant conversation.

His mother's room was down the hall from his, and she'd cornered him the second he had reached the top of the stairs.

"Come to my sitting room for some tea," she had insisted, and who was he to deny her?

Whatever small number of redeeming qualities he possessed, they had come from his mother. If there was decency in him (which was debatable), it was due to her influence. She'd tempered his father's hardness with softness. Brushed away the late duke's snide criticism with gentle compliments. Helped to coax out the bitterness when it threatened to sour him against the life he'd been given. A life most would kill to have, and rightly so. To be a duke in a time of political and social unrest was to be nigh on untouchable. But it wasn't all roses.

There was pain there. Mountains of it. Built up over years of being talked down to, and mocked, and derided. If not for his mother to show him that there was still kindness to be had, there wasn't a doubt in Perth's mind that he'd be even more of a cynical bastard than he already was.

And so, if she approached him and asked for his company while she indulged in a sober nightcap, then he wasn't going to refuse her. Even though two minutes after sitting down, he very much wished that he had.

"What is your opinion of the Rosewood girls?" she inquired without preamble.

"They have a loud rooster." He poured himself a cup of tea, then added a liberal splash of brandy. "And their house is falling apart."

"It does appear to be in a gradual state of disrepair," the dowager duchess allowed. "Not unexpected, given that their brother has been traveling abroad and they have been in mourning. I am sure once Lord Clarenmore returns, he will see to the renovations. An estate of this size is far too grand an undertaking for a woman to handle on her own, particularly when she is busy looking after her sisters."

"You mean Lenora." He cleared his throat. Sipped his tea. Then corrected himself in the hopes that his mother hadn't noticed the familiar air with which he spoke of their hostess. "Lady Lenora."

"Yes." A fond smile touched the corners of Anastasia's thin lips. "She is the very image of her mother. Lady Clarenmore had the same black hair and serious way about her. When she set her mind to something, there was nothing she could not achieve."

That sounded like Lenora.

Obstinate, headstrong, and stubborn.

So damned stubborn.

He'd gone out of his way to avoid her over these past few days. It hadn't been easy. She was bloody everywhere. And even when she wasn't, her perfume had a way of lingering in her wake. Especially now that he knew, intimately, how alluring her scent was.

Lilacs in spring.

She smelled like lilacs in spring…with a touch of citrus.

It was an intoxicating combination.

Sweet and sultry.

Much like Lenora herself.

Maybe a tad light on the sweet, as he'd met nicer badgers. But the sultry was there. She did a decent job at hiding it behind a disapproving frown and a stiff upper lip. But when he'd nibbled that lip, it had melted easily enough. Revealing that Lenora, for all her ice and snow, wasn't nearly as cold as she portrayed herself to be.

"You and Lady Lenora seemed to be having a delightful chat at dinner the other night." Anastasia eyed him over the rim of her porcelain teacup as she took a slow, thoughtful sip. "She is a remarkable young woman, is she not? Beautiful, intelligent, and poised."

"She's something all right," he muttered under his breath.

"I imagine that you would be hard pressed to find her equal if you searched the entire *ton*. Such a shame that she was made to cut her Season short and return here. She lost both her parents and whatever prospects she might have had, of which I am sure there were many. If not for tragedy, she'd most likely be married with a child."

Lenora?

Married?

Not so long ago, he'd felt a surge of pity for whatever poor fool ended up shackled to the blue-eyed ice queen. But that wasn't the emotion that stirred in his chest now when he pictured her with another man.

Being kissed by another man.

Having those purring sounds coaxed from her throat

by another man.

Writhing on a bench while another man knelt down between her thighs.

Jealousy struck hard and fast; a punch to his gut and another to his jaw. If they were physical blows, he'd have been rocked right off his feet. Knocked flat by an imaginary husband that didn't even exist. Married to a woman that he didn't even like.

Bollocks.

What the hell was happening to him?

"Are feeling all right, dear?" Anastasia asked. "You look peakish."

"I'm fine," he said flatly.

"If you wish to discuss it–"

"There is nothing to discuss." He finished his tea. Resisted the urge to slam the delicate cup on a table, and set it down with precise care instead. "Are you ready to return home yet? This house party is a bore, and it's not showing any signs of improvement."

The dowager duchess merely pulled a blanket over her lap. "It is half past ten, Perth. The horses are sleeping. Maybe you should be, too. It might do wonders for your demeanor. I hope you don't mind me saying, but you've been a bit of a grouch lately."

"Me?" he said incredulously. "Have you spoken to Lenora? I'm a balmy ray of sunshine compared to that storm cloud."

"Lady Lenora has conducted herself with incredible

grace under difficult circumstances. But now that you mention it, I have noticed a sort of tension between you two. I wonder why that is?" she mused. "You usually get along so well with the ladies. Occasionally *too* well, I should add. I guess you get that from your father. He was charming, if nothing else."

Perth stiffened. "I am nothing like him."

Anastasia smiled sadly. "So you have set out your entire life to prove."

"What the devil is that supposed to mean?"

She smoothed a wrinkle from the blanket. "It is not weakness to admit that your father hurt you, my darling boy. I tried to protect you when I could, but I fear that I failed more times than I succeeded. One of my greatest regrets."

"You did your best. He hurt you, too." And Perth hadn't been able to stop it. The old guilt, guilt that he'd done his best to forget, came rushing to the forefront. As did all the times he had seen his father put his hands on his mother. Never a slap, or an outright hit. That would be too obvious. Too beneath the wily viciousness of the Duke of Monmouth. But he'd left bruises all the same. On her wrists, that she concealed with gloves. On her neck, that she covered with scarves. And on her heart.

Especially on her heart.

Thrice, he'd intervened. Once when he was a lad of five. Far too young and too brave to know that he didn't stand a chance. His father had sent him crashing into a bookshelf with a casual swipe of his arm.

He tried again when he was twelve. Not too long after his boat was destroyed, and a piece of his boyhood along with it. He walked in to find his mother and father fighting. Hot, heated words that had crawled down his neck like ants. Monmouth had spat in his mother's face, and as Perth had watched the white saliva drip across her proud cheek, a red haze had overcome him.

All he remembered was charging, and then blackness.

Knocked out cold, his mother told him later as she'd held a compress to his throbbing temple. And gently scolded him for losing control.

"It's the one thing you have that he doesn't," she'd whispered. "Your father cannot control his rage, and that makes him even angrier because he knows it is a symptom of weakness. You must be strong, Perth. Stronger than him. Stronger than me. Stronger than both of us."

The third time he had finally, finally been a man full grown. On break from Eton, he had found himself at odds with his father over some ridiculous slight or another. The duke had started to berate him, just as he'd done a hundred times over. But this time, he didn't get to finish. And he spent the next two weeks indoors lest anyone see his black eye and ask him where he got it.

"Yes, he did hurt me." The dowager duchess permitted a brief mist of tears to enter her eyes, then blinked them away. "Monmouth was a cruel bully. I wish I had seen that in him before I fell in love, but then I never would have had you. My greatest pride, and the source of my joy. Without you, I don't know what might have become of me."

Perth reached for his empty teacup. He needed something tangible to hold. Something to shove all of these aching, unwanted emotions into. Haunting ghosts from a childhood that he didn't want to remember, and had done everything in his power to forget. "Mother–"

"Let me have my say," she said firmly. "There is no telling how many more of these heartfelt discussions we'll be able to have. I am not as young as I once was, and every year you become more resistant to listening to the wisdom of your elders."

"You're not an elder," he scoffed.

His mother, old?

Impossible.

But when he made himself look at her–not through the lens of a boy who had memorized her face in infancy, but as a detached adult gazing dispassionately upon the countenance of a stranger–he grudgingly acknowledged that she *was* growing old. As all people did. Life was a circle, not a straight, unyielding line. For some the circle was large. Others, small. But no matter their size, the circles always came back round eventually. Ashes to ashes, and dust to dust.

"I am," she said steadily. "I am, and one day, sooner than we'd both like, I will no longer be here."

"Are you trying to ruin my night?" he wondered aloud. "Because you don't have to put this much effort into it. In case you hadn't noticed, I almost had to attend a recital today. I'm already miserable."

Anastasia's eyes glittered with amusement. "Then you missed a lovely playing of Bach's *Fugue in G minor*. I'd never heard it on a pianoforte before. Lady Bridget did a wonderful job. She is quite talented. But then, so was her mother."

"I'll make certain to watch the next one."

"I'm sure." His mother sighed. "What I am *trying* to tell you is that while you and your father share some characteristics, you're right. You aren't Monmouth. You could never be him. You have a heart. A conscience. There is goodness in you, as much as you attempt to hide it. Which means you need not worry that if you take a wife, and father a child, you will somehow turn into the monster that he was."

Perth expelled a ragged breath. "That isn't why I haven't married."

Except it was.

Deep down, it *was* the reason.

The reason for his cavalier attitude. His sly commentary. His curt indifference. All in an effort to keep everyone else at arm's length. Not to protect him from them, but to save *them* from *him*. It was why he did not form attachments. Why his mistresses never occupied his bed for more than a month or two before he paid them handsomely to be on their way. Why he took such great pains to avoid any female that had the makings of a duchess. Not because he found ladies of the *ton* to be vain, boring, vapid creatures who only cared about wealth and appearance…all right, yes he did. But *mostly* because he didn't want to fall in love.

He didn't want to fall in love, and become his father.

The late Duke of Monmouth was a rotten apple born of a decaying tree. As his sire had been, and his sire before him, and his sire before him.

Why should Perth believe that he was any different?

Maybe he'd never felt inclined to strike a member of the fairer sex, or even speak harshly to her. But that didn't mean that he wouldn't. That didn't mean there wasn't the same rot sloshing around inside of him. Just waiting to spill out. And the only way to keep it contained was to remain alone.

If he didn't marry, then he couldn't hurt his wife as his father had hurt his mother.

It was as simple as that.

"There *is* goodness in you," the dowager duchess repeated. "If you cannot see it, then you need to find someone who can. Goodnight, my dear."

Perth dutifully kissed his mother on the cheek, then sought his bed. But it was a long, long while before he managed to fall asleep.

# 12

### *Leaky Pipes*

LENORA ROSE EVEN EARLIER than usual the next morning. Weary from a restless night's sleep, but determined to meet whatever challenges the day brought her head on, she donned a plain green dress sans crinoline (a formal gown of sea blue interwoven with strips of gold silk was already laid out and waiting for the opera performance after dinner), swept her hair into a bun, and set forth to conquer the world. Or, if not the world, then at least Clarenmore Park.

With the day barely woken and the sunrise still a sleepy murmur of pale pink, she pulled on her gloves and marched downstairs…straight into chaos.

"My lady! Praise be that you are here." Mrs. Weidman, the housekeeper, came rushing over with a glazed look of what could only be described as panic in her eyes. As she was ordinarily a stalwart woman who had served the Rosewoods for nearly three decades and had rarely encountered any concern, large or small, that she was incapable of handling without assistance, this was a cause for alarm.

"What is it?" Lenora asked, stepping down off the bottom stair. Her head swiveled and her nostrils flared as she looked all around, half expecting to see flames shooting out of the parlor or shattered glass littering the floor from a fallen chandelier. "What's wrong?"

"The fountains have stopped working," Mrs. Weidman wailed.

"Oh." She breathed an audible sigh of relief. "That's no reason to–"

"The water's backed up into the kitchens! It's flooded to the work tables, my lady. All the food that was prepared for this morning's breakfast is destroyed."

"Then we'll have to go into the pantry and–"

"That's flooded too! And the cellars." Mrs. Weidman threw her hands in the air. "Cook is threatening to quit, three of my maids are under the weather, we've lost another livery boy, and the next shipment of goods has been delayed due to nonpayment on the last one."

Well that explained the panic, then.

"I am sorry, my lady." Tears filled the housekeeper's merry blue eyes. "I've failed you. Your mother would be so disappointed in me. Poor Lady Clarenmore is probably rolling in her grave. To have her–"

"Mrs. Weidman. Mrs. Weidman!" Lenora placed her hands on the housekeeper's shoulders and gave her a shake. She'd never witnessed the servant in such a state before, but it wasn't entirely surprising. They had all been strained as of late. For the past year and a half, really. Ever since James had left on his Grand Tour, things had started to go wrong. Or to break. Or to fall into ruin.

She'd done her best to fill in the gaps, to patch the holes, to procure money that wasn't there. To continue plowing ahead as if nothing was amiss while knowing full well that it was going to catch up with them eventually.

It appeared that eventually was now. In the middle of the house party, no less. Because of course, of course, *of course* that damned plumbing that James had insisted they spend a small fortune on to have installed would break.

On today, of all days.

"Have any other rooms flooded?" she asked. "Have any of the guests been impacted?"

"No, my lady." Mrs. Weidman used her apron to pat her cheeks dry. "There's a water closet that's a foot under, but no one uses it anyway. The water's started to recede. Mr. Barnaby managed to find the main valve and shut it off. He's down there now, trying to figure out what went wrong. We'd send for a plumber, but…"

They didn't have anything to pay him with.

Lenora had not been tutored in finances and bookkeeping and crop rotations. Which was why it had taken her so long to find out that Clarenmore Park had been losing money for years. Bad investments, coupled with a dishonest accountant, coupled with a terrible drought, coupled with their father being (rightfully) more concerned with the health of his ailing wife than the coffers of his ailing estate had all contributed to the inescapable fact that the Rosewoods were all but destitute.

Even her sisters didn't realize the full extent of it. She hadn't wanted to burden them. And she hadn't wanted to *be* burdened any more than she already was. By all the questions they'd ask, and the solutions they'd offer. Solutions that would ultimately fail, because she'd tried them already.

There was nothing left to be done.

No point in worrying over what couldn't be fixed.

Her main focus had been, and continued to be, on seeing her sisters settled into marriages with husbands who'd never need worry about being able to afford to pay a plumber to fix broken pipes. That was why this Season was so important. Why it meant so much. Time was *not* on the side of the Rosewoods. If James did not soon return, it would be a race to see whether they completely ran out of money or Richard took what little they had left. Either way, they would lose.

"We'll do fresh bowls of fruit straight from the garden," she told Mrs. Weidman. "There's raspberries left. Blueberries as well. And it's early yet, but I'm sure we can put together a bushel or two of apples from the orchard. I can fetch those myself. Did water get into the icebox?"

"I don't think so, my lady."

"Then we'll have cream, too. Eggs from the henhouse. And I'll send Annie to collect fresh loaves of bread from the baker. Mr. Gentry is an old family friend, and hasn't yet attempted to collect on the debt we owe." She glanced at the tall case clock in the corner of the foyer. "It'll be another three hours before anyone else is up. When they do make their way downstairs, we shall welcome them with the simple charm of a country breakfast."

"But what of dinner?" Mrs. Weidman fretted. "Cook has been braising the mutton since yesterday morning and it's soaked through. There's not enough time to begin again."

"Then we shall have to come up with something else, won't we?" Lenora summoned a smile. "Have Mr. Barnaby continue working on the pipes. If memory serves, Tom the footman worked in a hotel in Bath before he came here. I'm sure they had their fair share of plumbing troubles. Maybe he'll know what to do."

"You're right, my lady. And wise, besides." Tears glinted in the housekeeper's eyes once again, albeit for a different reason. "If you don't mind me saying, Lady

Clarenmore would be so proud of you. For the way you've handled yourself in the face of all these troubles, and taken care of your sisters besides."

"Thank you, Mrs. Weidman." When her smile threatened to crack and her resolve to break, Lenora rubbed her hands briskly together. She couldn't afford to crumble. Falling apart was a luxury reserved for those who didn't have a kitchen three feet under water and a house filled with twenty-five of their peers. "I'll get those apples now."

"Oh, no, my lady. Let me send a maid!"

"Keep the maids here," she instructed. "You said we're already down two. The comfort of our guests is paramount. I'd like another dusting of the front parlor, and fresh linens put on all the beds in the west wing. The flowers in the music room could also stand to be replaced. Not to mention the ballroom must be ready for tonight. The maids will be busy enough. The least I can do is gather apples. Besides, I'd like a walk. I need to stretch my legs."

"If you're sure…" the housekeeper trailed off.

"Positive. While the kitchen is airing out, let's have Cook move her staff to the old summer house. It's clean, and there's already tables there with plenty of room. Cook won't like it"–a Frenchwoman with a notoriously difficult temperament, Mrs. Bouchard was at Clarenmore Park for the simple reason that no other household would have her–"but it is the best we can do."

"Let me handle Cook and all the rest." Her confidence returned, Mrs. Weidman retied her apron strings and straightened her mobcap, then clicked her heels together. "When you return with the apples, I'll have the house running like clockwork, my lady. You need not worry about a thing."

Lenora knew *that* wasn't true, but what choice did she have but to smile and nod as if it were? She'd never been on a grand sailing schooner, and had no plans to follow in her brother's footsteps and set sail across the ocean anytime soon. But she imagined that if the captain of such a vessel started to run around and shout that they were sinking, it would only lead to more chaos.

A steady captain, a seasoned captain, a reliable captain remained calm even when the bow was going under and the rats had begun to flee. He ensured his crew and his passengers were safely in their lifeboats and then he rode out the storm on the deck. Risking his own life, if necessary, to protect what was most precious. Never running. Never flinching. Never letting on that he was a hairs breadth from diving into the crashing sea and swimming for his life.

"I have my full faith in you, Mrs. Weidman."

It was herself that she was starting to doubt.

"LADY LENORA." The Viscount Croft greeted her before she'd made it halfway to the orchards. A light sheen of perspiration clung to his forehead, indicating that he was at the end of his morning constitutional. "The very person I was hoping to run across."

"Oh no." Her shoulders slumped. "What's wrong now?"

"Nothing that I am aware of." Stern lines bracketed the corners of Lord Croft's unsmiling mouth. "I merely wanted to take the opportunity to ask your permission to court Lady Bridget. I would ask your brother, were he here. Since he is not, I assumed the most proper thing to do would to present the question to you, my lady."

Proper.

What a refreshing word to hear.

Perth could learn a thing or two from Lord Croft, she thought. Although admittedly, there was something about the viscount's stiff cordiality that was a tad…off-putting. He was almost *too* polite. If there even was such a thing. But that did not change the fact that Lord Croft was both a respectable gentleman and a personal friend of James'. In sending him an invitation, she had secretly hoped that he might express interest in one of her sisters. Annabel, perhaps. Or maybe Eloise. The wild redhead would surely benefit from some stiff cordiality. She hadn't even considered Bridget. But it seemed that Lord Croft had.

"Your children?" she inquired politely, slanting a hand across her brow to block out the rising sun. "They are well?"

"Indeed. Sebastian and Violet are staying at Rutland Crossing for the duration of the summer. By all accounts, they are enjoying themselves immensely."

"That's wonderful to hear." She paused, the toe her boot digging into freshly raked dirt as she considered the best way to proceed without paying insult to Bridget *or* Lord Croft. To the best of her knowledge, Bridget had never mentioned the viscount before. She was almost certainly unaware that he was interested in pursuing a relationship with her. Why, then, this sudden request for a courtship? Unless something had occurred that Lenora was not privy too. Had Bridget and Lord Croft visited the same bench as she and Perth?

When a blush teased the nape of her neck, she found herself grateful that she'd had the foresight to drape a shawl over her shoulders before departing the house.

"Have you spoken to my sister, my lord? Is she aware of your...objective?" She did not wish to pester the viscount unduly, or look a gift horse in the mouth. But neither would she consign her sister to a courtship with a man who was not genuinely committed to marriage. Bridget's heart was tender and easily bruised. She wanted romance, not a casual dalliance. If the viscount's sudden attentiveness wasn't rooted in good intentions, then Lenora would not encourage it.

Lord Croft delivered a curt nod. "We have exchanged pleasantries."

"And…it went well?"

"Indeed."

She pursed her lips. She had never attempted to extract information from a sphinx before, but she was fairly confident it would be a breeze compared to getting anything out of the viscount.

"What is it, in particular, that you like about my sister?"

"What do I like about her?" he said blankly.

"Yes. There must be some specific traits that you admire." She smiled encouragingly. "Her love of reading, perhaps? Or her musical skills. She is quite adept at the pianoforte, is she not?"

Lord Croft tugged at the collar of his jacket and frowned. Despite the early hour and the vigorousness of his walk, he was fully dressed in a burgundy frock coat, tie, vest, and stove pipe trousers. The only item of clothing he'd gone without was a hat. His hair, a medium brown with streaks of wheat from the sun, was tied back the sharp, angular planes of his face with a strip of leather. "I like that Lady Bridget is quiet. She does not partake in gossip, or chatter incessantly."

"Bridget does prefer to keep to herself. If she were to choose between a book and ball, the book would always win." Lenora studied Lord Croft intently. He'd not given her very much information or insight into his character. But there was something–an errant feeling, an instinct– that told her to trust him.

The viscount may have been a man of few words, but it appeared, to her, at least, that he was a man of high moral character. As those seemed fewer and farer between these days, she saw no reason to deny his request.

"So long as my sister is obliging, then you have my blessing to pursue a courtship." She clasped her hands together. "It is honorable that you would ask for my permission, Lord Croft. I am grateful that you would make such a consideration."

"Thank you, my lady." His countenance devoid of expression, he gave another clipped nod. "I have every reason to believe that Lady Bridget and I will be remarkably suited for each other."

*But what of passion and love and lust,* a small voice intruded.

Lenora batted it away.

As she'd told her sisters last night in the Crescent Room, a marriage built on nothing more than a foundation of desire was sure to topple. An eternal union between two people needed sturdy blocks comprised of loyalty and dedication. *Not* kisses in hallways. Why, just look at the viscount's first marriage!

If the rumors were to be trusted, he'd chosen the mother of his children based on nothing *but* desire. A black mark against him, to be sure, although he'd repaired his reputation admirably. Enough so that he was out here, formally requesting her approval before he so much as held a door open for Bridget.

Meanwhile, Perth was running about thrusting his tongue into whatever crevice he could find. With no thought of courtship, or marriage, or what might have happened to *her* reputation had they been discovered!

The differences between the two men couldn't have been more apparent. Lord Croft was a gentleman, through and through. Whereas Perth was the definition of a rogue. She was willing to bet five shillings that if she opened a dictionary and flipped to R, there he'd be. Grinning back at her. Not a hint of repentance in those deep, rich, velvety brown eyes of his.

He was the *worst* possible choice for a husband.

She wouldn't recommend him to her worst enemy.

Despite that, if she stood the Duke of Monmouth and Lord Croft side by side, only one of them would make her heart beat a little faster.

And it wasn't the viscount.

*Infatuation*, she told herself.

She was suffering from a mild case of infatuation.

That's all it was.

By depriving herself of Perth and his rakish attention, she'd unintentionally exacerbated her symptoms. Maybe what she really needed to do was purge him from her system once and for all. Eat all the chocolate cake in a single go, so that it wasn't down in the kitchen waiting for her. Calling to her. Tempting her to have just *one* more bite.

Because even after the house party ended, their paths would continue to inevitably cross. Especially given that she and her sisters would be making their grand return to Society.

She'd see Perth at balls. At charity dinners. At the theater.

When that occurred, she did not want her heart to race or her pulse to quicken. Instead, she yearned to feel what she always had whenever she'd happened to catch a glimpse of him.

Apathy entwined with mild disgust.

She missed that reaction!

And she wanted it back.

It was infinitely more convenient to loathe Perth than to love him.

So perhaps...perhaps she *did* need to give in to temptation.

Temporarily, that is.

Lick all the crumbs off her plate and be done with it.

Done with *him* and these meddling feelings that she hadn't asked for.

"I should...I should continue on before the other guests arise." *And I don't have any food to give them.* "But I'll ensure that you and Bridget are seated next to each other at dinner tonight." *If there is a dinner.* "I wish you luck in your endeavor, my lord. All I ask is that you treat my sister with kindness." *She'll need it when we're all homeless.* "Hers is a gentle spirit, and I'd not wish to have her hurt in any way."

The viscount's cheeks reddened. The first display of emotion that he'd shown. "I am sure that you are aware of my history, as if everyone else in the *ton*. But I can grant you all assurances that where Lady Bridget is concerned, I shall tread with infinite care and respect. I am not only seeking a wife, but a mother for my children. In that regard, I take this matter extremely seriously."

"I did not mean to infer otherwise, Lord Croft." She curtsied, then hurried on her way.

# 13

## *Orgasms in the Orchard*

THE FUCKING ROOSTER was at it again.

"God*damnit* Sir Kensington," Perth cursed as he stomped down the stairs two at a time, his shirt only partially buttoned and his black frockcoat thrown over his arm. "You're going in a bloody pot this time and that's all there is to it."

Scrubbing a hand across his face in an attempt to wipe the sleep from his eyes, he glowered at a maid as she scurried past carrying a tin bucket overflowing with raspberries. Another followed close behind, this one holding a bucket of blueberries. To his bemusement, he noted that their skirts were soaked from the knee down. The same with the footman who came forward to address him, his shoes making squishing sounds as he hurried across the foyer.

"Can I fetch you anything, Your Grace?" asked the footman, his young, earnest face dotted with freckles. "Coffee, or a carriage brought round? I am afraid breakfast isn't ready yet."

"I can see that." Perth rested his elbow on the newel post at the base of the stairs. "What the devil is going on? Why are you all wet? Why's everyone running around like chickens with their heads cut of?" Speaking of which… "You don't happen to know where I can get an axe, do you? A proper axe. Not a knife."

The footman blanched. "An…an axe, Your Grace?"

It was, Perth allowed, an unusual request for a duke to make.

Especially at half past six in the morning.

But it wasn't *his* fault that he was up this early.

"Where is Lady Lenora?" he demanded. "I've a murder to commit and I'd like to get on with it so that I can return to my bed."

The footman's knobby Adam's apple gave a jerk. "You-you want an axe and to know the whereabouts of Lady Lenora, Your Grace?"

"Yes. Wait. It's not what it sounds like. The rooster. I'm going to kill the *rooster* with the axe. Not Lady Lenora. I just need *her* to find *him*."

"Sir Kensington?" the footman ventured.

"Yes, Sir Kensington," Perth said impatiently. "The feathered bane of my existence. He's crowed his last crow, I'm afraid. Best say your goodbyes now."

"I'm sorry he has woken you up, Your Grace. But he's a good rooster," the footman said earnestly. "Takes care of his flock, wards off the hawks, and doesn't go after anyone."

"I shall be sure to give him a fair trial and the opportunity to plead his case before the execution." Perth arched a brow. "I take it you'd like to stand in as a witness on behalf of the accused?"

The footman nodded. "I would, Your Grace."

"Excellent. An axe, if you'd be so kind."

"But…" The footman shuffled his feet and scratched his chin, which by the look of it had yet to see its first whisker. "But why would you need an axe if a verdict hasn't yet been reached?"

"Because I'm going to chop off its head."

"Respectfully, Your Grace, that doesn't seem like much of a fair trial."

"Is this an actual conversation that I'm having?" Perth wondered aloud. "Never mind the axe, then. Just point me in the direction of Lady Lenora."

"She was headed toward the orchards last I saw her." This from Graham, who strode into the foyer already dressed and impeccably groomed. He stopped beside the footman and frowned. "Are you aware that your trousers are wet?"

"There was an incident with the plumbing. All the kitchen's flooded. The cellars, too."

"Is the wine all right?" Perth asked, vaguely alarmed.

"To the best of my knowledge, Your Grace."

"Thank God for small favors." He shrugged into his coat. "The orchards, did you say?"

"Indeed," said Graham.

"Is it a far walk?"

"No more than half a mile."

Perth almost choked. "Half a *mile?*"

"If the physical requirements of such a meager distance are too great, I am sure you can send someone with a message in your stead," Graham said blandly.

"I'd be happy to go, Your Grace," offered the footman.

Perth regarded them both with narrowed eyes. "I did not rise from my bed at this uncivilized hour to be insulted. If Lady Lenora is in the orchard, then I'll bloody well walk to the orchard." He was halfway out the front door before he paused. "What way am I walking?"

The footman and the viscount pointed in unison.

"To the left," said Graham. "Follow the main path until it diverges, and then take the trail to the right past the stables and the milking barn. If you reach a pond, you've gone too far."

"Sounds easy enough." His gaze flicked to the footman. "If you come across Sir Kensington, let him know that his hours are numbered."

With that, he marched out of the house.

THERE ONCE WAS A TIME when Clarenmore Park had been renowned for its apple orchards. Originally planted by Lenora's great-great-great-grandfather, the fruit-bearing trees thrived in a sunny alcove to the south of the manor. Surrounded by a towering thicket that provided a natural windbreak and protection from deer, it was a magical place. Or so it had been before the infamous fire blight of 1805 took hold, devastating half the orchard and forcing Lenora's great-grandfather to start anew.

A scientific man by nature, the late Earl of Clarenmore had brought in a variety of American apple trees to toughen up the stock that had survived the blight. Through grafting, the curious act of splicing a detached stem from one tree and attaching it to another, he managed to create an entirely new subspecies of apple, a hardier combination of Winter Pearmain and New York Pippin.

The fruit that the trees yielded was sweet, had a longer harvesting season, and were suitable for both baking and eating fresh off the stem. Predictably, they were called Clarenmores, and since they were old enough to walk, Lenora and her siblings had been toddling out to the orchard to play hide-and-seek, or practice their climbing skills, or lay on a blanket and bet ginger candies on who would be hit in the head with a falling apple first.

There were over fifty trees in total, planted in orderly rows of ten. July was early for a crop to be ready. Normally the apples ripened towards the end of August and into September. But as she picked up a wooden crate and propped it against her hip, Lenora spied a flash of red peeking out through a cluster of shiny green leaves.

She'd collected over a dozen apples when she sensed someone behind her. In the process of standing on her toes in an attempt to snag an apple just out of reach, she didn't bother to turn around before she said, "Thank you for coming to help, but I told Mrs. Weidman it wasn't necessary to send someone."

A large, masculine hand reached past her and grabbed the apple. "Who is Mrs. Weidman?"

On a gasp of surprise, Lenora dropped onto her heels and whirled around. "You shouldn't sneak up on people like that! What are you even doing out here, anyway?" she demanded of Perth, who fueled the flames of her ire even higher when he sank his teeth into the apple and took a big, crunchy bite. "I needed that!"

"What are *you* doing here?" he countered, tossing the apple from one hand to the other. Like Lord Croft, he wasn't wearing a hat, and his dusky blond tresses appeared as if they'd yet to see a comb. His coat and shirt sleeves were rolled up, exposing his muscular forearms where a dusting of gold hair resided. He'd not bothered to tie his cravat and his vest was unbuttoned, contributing to his overall appearance of lazy dishevelment and offering a tantalizing glimpse of his neck, the skin bronzed from the sun and covered in a thin layer of sweat.

Her tongue passed across her bottom lip as heat curled in her belly. Traditionally, she'd found herself drawn to elegant, well-dressed men who took pride in their appearance and turn out. How was it, then, that the more clothes Perth chose not to wear, the more attracted to him she became?

*Cake*, she reminded herself.

*He's just a piece of cake.*

Drats.

That only made it worse.

"I…" She adjusted her grip on the crate as a corner of it jabbed painfully into her hipbone. "I came to collect apples. Clearly."

"Yes, but the question is why?" He took another bite, and the sight of those even white teeth sinking into the red flesh of the apple did…odd things to Lenora.

Slippery things.

*Lustful* things.

It was an indescribable feeling. The slight hitch of her breath. The quiet, tingling *hum* of her blood. The way her toes curled and the muscles on the inside of her thighs trembled.

The only comparison she had was when she walked into a room and everything was organized to perfection with nary a chair out of place.

And wasn't that pitiful?

That before Perth, the closest she'd ever come to all-consuming desire was a row of books in alphabetical order.

She blew out a stream of air, pushing away a curl that had come loose from her practical, matronly bun. "The apples are for breakfast. Cook will be serving a country-style arrangement of fresh fruit, eggs, and bread, along with a variety of jams, fresh butter, and cream. It's said to a personal favorite of Queen Victoria."

"While a 'country-style arrangement' sounds delightful, I fear the cat's out of the bag, as they say." He leaned against the tree and folded his arms over his mouthwateringly broad chest. "A servant told me the kitchen flooded."

"All right, yes," she said crossly. "The kitchen flooded and ruined all the food that was already prepared. Cook is up in arms. The mutton for tonight is ruined. Two maids are sick, and we haven't the means to employ any others. As it is, we cannot even afford to hire a plumber to fix the broken pipe! Our brother, James, isn't on some Grand Tour. He's missing. Most likely dead. Once our cousin figures it out, we'll lose our home and be out on the street without a shilling to our name. There! Is that what you wanted to hear?" She stopped, her chest heaving. Both from the amount of oxygen such a long tirade had demanded, and the sudden weight that had been lifted off it from revealing the truth. "Is that what you wanted to know? Clarenmore Park is in shambles, we're on the brink of financial ruin, James is gone, and there's nothing I can do to fix any of it except collect a bushel of these damned apples! So that is what I am doing."

An eerie sense of calm descended over Lenora as she showed Perth her back and returned to her work. On the surface, she was absolutely mortified that she'd just revealed her family's innermost secrets. To the Duke of Monmouth, of all people! But beneath that, she felt…she felt *relieved*. That someone else knew what she'd been hiding. Even if it was Perth.

She didn't jump when a hand rested on her shoulder and gently squeezed, but something inside of her loosened. Like a corset stay come undone, allowing her to finally breathe. The crate dropped to the ground. Apples rolled everywhere, but she paid them no heed. On a small whimper of need, she turned into the duke's arms and pressed her mouth to his.

He stilled for the time that it took for her heart to beat once.

A single *thump* against her ribcage.

And then his fingers were in her hair, and his tongue was between her lips, and his arousal was pushing against her belly. Hot, hard, and demanding. Its phallus-shaped outline branding her flesh even through the layers that she wore.

Her own hands streaked across his chest, diving under his shirt to touch the warm skin beneath. His pectoral muscles rippled in response, and when the gloved pads of her thumb–by accident instead of any planned sensual design–passed over his nipples, she was fascinated to discover that they were as sharp and pointed as the ends of a diamond.

He angled his head, deepening the kiss.

Passion thrummed inside of her, fighting to be released. To throw off the title of lady, and all that it implied. The manners. The politeness. The etiquette. The implication that if she wasn't well-behaved, if she didn't conduct herself in a certain way, if she failed to meet the expectations of others, then she was failing.

Failing herself. Failing her peers. Failing her parents.

But who could be perfect all the time?

Who would *want* to be?

Especially when being wicked was so much more rewarding.

The stubble of a jaw unshaven scraped against her throat as Perth dragged his mouth down her neck to her shoulder. He nipped her there, then suckled. Hard enough to form a bruise that would be covered by her dress, but she would know of its existence in the days to come. And in the knowing, she'd have a reminder that when she relinquished control…when she relinquished control, she was able to embrace the wantonness that dwelled within her.

Waiting, all this time waiting, to be set free.

Her hands rose from his torso to rake through his hair,

her head lolling to the side on a moan of ecstasy when his attention went to her breasts. Her dress, several years old and the fabric stretched thin from too many washings, easily gave way when his nimble fingers plucked at the mother of pearl buttons running the length of her spine. The sleeves slid down to her wrists and the bodice slithered to her waist, leaving her wearing nothing more than a boned corset over a cotton chemise.

An impatient yank and the corset was torn away.

Perth lowered his mouth to her nipple, already taut and aching.

"Poor minx," he murmured, massaging the underside of her breast as he tilted the swollen rosebud to his lips. "Look what that evil contraption has done to you."

Lenora couldn't look. Not without stepping out of his arms, and she'd rather jump into a freezing cold lake than do that. But then, she didn't need to. She was fully aware of the red lines that crisscrossed her skin from the rigid edges of the corset. Lines that never faded. Not completely. Because every time they were near to disappearing, she rose from her bed and strapped herself into the corset all over again.

And if that wasn't an analogy, what was?

Weeks, months, years, *decades* of always doing what she ought to. Of wearing that blasted corset day in and day out, and her crinoline besides. Of literally caging herself in. But for what? She had done everything that she was supposed to. She had followed every rule to the letter. She had memorized *The True Ladies Manual of Politeness and Etiquette.* And yet despite her best efforts, her parents were still dead. Her sisters were still unmarried. Her brother was still missing. Clarenmore Park was still tumbling into disrepair.

What had obeying the rules gotten her, except for marks on her skin and a wall of pent up frustrations so high that it nearly reached the sky?

Nothing.

It hadn't gotten her a damned thing.

Whereas breaking the one cardinal rule that young ladies were told they *must* adhere to…that had given her pleasure. That had provided her with release. That had shown her a glimpse of ecstasy she hadn't even known existed. And she wanted more of it. She wanted *all* of it. Maybe stoking the flames of her desire was wrong, but at least when she was burning she didn't feel cold. At least when she was burning, she felt *alive.*

Perth gave her that. He also gave her a headache from grinding her teeth over every outlandish statement that came out of his mouth, but more importantly–most importantly–he gave her life. He gave her lust. And maybe…just maybe…he gave her lo–

"*Oh,*" she cried out when he teased her nipple with his tongue.

Her chemise was gone. She didn't know when, or how. It had simply…vanished. Along with the rest of her inhibitions.

The shock of Perth's mouth directly on her naked breast sent a sizzling punch of heat straight to her loins. Her skirts, bunched around her hips, rustled as she pushed her quivering thighs together. She might have slid to the ground in a boneless pile of limbs and lust had Perth not lowered her there first.

He whipped off his coat and spread it under her like a blanket, cocooning her in his scent.

"Lift your hips," he ordered roughly, and when she complied he stripped off her gown and drawers and tossed them to the side.

Dressed in sunlight and a streak of shadow from the tree above them, her hands crept in to cover herself, but Perth stilled them with his own, thumbs pressing lightly on the madly fluttering beat of her pulses.

"Don't." His eyes were dark, his voice hoarse. "I want to look at you."

Another order.

Another command.

She obeyed this as she had the last. For someone who told others what to do–maids, footmen, her sisters–it was secretly thrilling to surrender to Perth's demands. To give him the control she ordinarily reserved for herself. To let him do with her what he willed.

Fully clothed, he climbed atop of her, the heels of his hands sinking into the grass on either side of her head as his knees straddled her hips in an intimate embrace.

A quick peak between his legs noted the size and

bulge of his arousal. Fully erect, Perth's cock threatened to push out of the fall front of his trousers. A bead of moisture had soaked through the moleskin, forming an uneven circle of dampness.

As his gaze slowly traveled from the tangled waves of her hair to the curls below her navel, Lenora bit her bottom lip. Her heart was a train inside her chest, clattering along the tracks at breakneck speed. Courtesy of a book and the wagging tongue of Miss Agnes Bulwark, she had a rudimentary concept of what lovemaking entailed. That was to say, she was aware of where a male's genitalia went during sexual relations. But confronted with the sheer *size* of Perth's phallus, she was made to wonder if the lewd images in the book had been as accurate as she'd once believed.

All that, go in *her?*

Impossible.

It'd never fit.

As if he could read her mind, Perth chuckled quietly under his breath, then bent his head and nuzzled the hollow in the middle of her sternum. "I like what you're thinking, minx. But as much as I'd love to sheath myself in that tight, wet little quim, we'll not go that far. I am nothing if not a gentleman."

His words, huskily uttered, ignited a spark within her. A spark that erupted into a roaring flame when he continued down her body to the apex of her thighs…and licked.

"You're–you're not a gentleman at all," she gasped, her shoulder blades shoving into the hard earth as she arched off his coat.

"Regretfully, in this particular instance, I seem to be." His mouth tickled her as he hovered right above her thatch of ebony curls. Nibbling, kissing, licking everywhere but *there*, where she wanted him the most. Then he bent his head and took seriously to his work, stopping only to push her legs apart whenever they began to fold inward.

This time she knew where the ascent was leading. Where that mountain trail was taking her. And how glorious it would be when she reached the top. But Perth, scoundrel that he was, drove her up to the peak…then left her to linger there, her head thrashing from side to side as her muscles clenched in anticipation of what remained frustratingly out of reach.

Again, and again, and *again* he brought her right to the edge. Mercilessly teasing her with release even as his mouth retreated and he lazily stroked her belly instead.

"*Perth*." She had never used his Christian name before. But this hardly seemed like the moment for formalities. "I…I…"

"Yes?" He lifted his head, revealing a mouth shiny from her secretions and eyes glittering with carnal humor. "Is there something I can help you with?"

She squirmed, restless in her unsated desire. "I want to…to feel what I did before. In the hallway."

He swirled his index finger and his thumb in his mouth, then pinched her nipple. "Can you be more specific?"

"N-no," she moaned when he wet his fingers again, and did the same to her other nipple. Her arms reached out to the side, mindlessly tearing up handfuls of grass as he continued to torment her in the most delicious ways possible.

"You want to come. That's what it's called, Lenora. That feeling deep inside. Of pure, unadulterated bliss." His mouth skimmed across her abdomen to the point of her hip. He traced the crescent-shaped protrusion with his tongue, then raised his head once more, his gaze as velvety black as the devil's himself. "Tell me. Tell me what you want me to do.

She pursed her lips, struggling to form the words. "I want...I want to come. I want you to make me come."

"Perth," he growled. "Say it."

"I want you to make me come...*Perth!*" A cry of abandon wrenched itself free from the very base of her throat when he thrust his tongue all the way inside of her while simultaneously rolling a single fingertip across the sensitive pearl nestled amidst her slick curls.

The result was instantaneous. She came immediately, with even more force than before. The sheer explosion of it left her reeling, and she could have sworn she saw spots dancing in front of her eyes when she squeezed them shut and reflexively clamped her thighs around Perth's shoulders, holding her to him until every last quiver had left her body.

In the aftermath she lay dazed, hardly able to comprehend what had happened. Then her brow knit with concern. Heedless of her nudity–when a man did *that* to a woman, she could hardly cling to a false sense of modesty–she sat up on her elbows with a troubled expression. "I did...that is, I...I..."

"Came. Or orgasmed, if you'd prefer to be proper." A rakish grin captured his mouth. "I know how proper you like to be, minx."

The second word might have been the correct terminology but it *sounded* dirtier, filthy even, and thus she used the first, even managing to insert a note of primness into her tone as her wits gradually returned despite being sprawled naked on a duke's coat in broad daylight.

"I came. But...but you didn't?" She snuck a swift glance below his waist to be sure...and her eyes widened when she saw that, impossibly, he'd grown even *larger* than he was before.

"No, I didn't." Perth sat on his knees, legs brazenly spread and hands resting on his thighs. Watching her, he canted his head to the side. "Does that concern you, Lady Lenora?"

Oh, so it was Lady Lenora again, was it?

She nearly snorted at the hypocrisy. Sobered when of its own accord, her curious stare once more slid to his nether regions. "Does it hurt? To be…to be that engorged."

"It's not the most comfortable thing in the world," he said dryly, "but I'll find a way to survive."

"Is…is there anything I can…" Her face reddened. "Do?"

Perth's gaze went from lazy amusement to rapt fascination in the blink of an eye.

"Aye," he said, his voice barely registering above a croak. "There is. If you are so inclined."

"I am," she whispered as a different sort of delight, the kind that came from giving a gift rather than receiving it, shimmered through her.

"Well, then." His hands went to his trousers. Never taking his gaze off her, he began the process of unfastening them. "Give me your hand…"

# 14

### *Duly Noted*

IF THIS WAS heaven, Perth thought as he watched Lenora's hand slowly stroke the length of his cock, then he needed to find a priest to absolve him of his past misdeeds immediately, because he was damned if he was going to spend an eternity in hell.

He was on his back with her curled beside him, her silken skin dappled in shadow. A light breeze stirred the air, rustling the leaves overhead and carrying with it the sweet scent of fruit and the sharper, fuller tang of sex.

Sweat gathered on his brow and his stomach clenched as his bollocks began to tighten. Lenora had barely started, and already he was about to spend himself like a virgin romping about in the hayloft with the village barmaid.

He was hard as a railroad pike.

All veins and swollen flesh and a light sheen of dampness at the tip.

"Am I doing it right?" she asked softly, pausing with her hand at the base of his throbbing shaft. Her fingers almost encircled him all the way around, and when she gave a light, tentative squeeze his hips shot off the ground.

"Yes," he managed hoarsely. "God, yes."

She stroked him again, and again, instinctively increasing her speed as his breaths grew raspier and his eyes rolled towards the back of his head. Without being instructed, she used her other hand to cup his bollocks...and he lost control.

Perth Robert Stewart, 8th Duke of Monmouth and lover extraordinaire, released his seed on a gruff shout as a wave of indescribable pleasure washed over him, ensnared him in its powerful grip, and then tossed him back out to sea where he paddled, panting, in ever widening circles until he was drawn into the shore on the tide to find a raven-haired siren waiting to greet him on the rocky cliffside.

She dared a glance at him beneath a sweep of sultry lashes, blushed, and quickly looked away. "Did you...ah, that is to say..."

"I came hard enough to tilt the globe off its axis," he groaned, folding his arms behind his head and enjoying the sort of solid, bone-popping stretch that only followed an orgasm. "If that's what you were asking. I just wish it had lasted longer."

"I'm sorry." She blinked at him, then frowned. "As you can probably imagine, I've never done that before, and–"

"The fault is entirely mine, minx." He slanted a hand above his brow to guard his eyes from a sharp slice of sunlight and grinned at her. "Next time I'll be more prepared."

"*Next time?*" she squeaked adorably. "Oh, I don't think–"

"Let's get dressed," he interrupted, not wanting to give her clever mind the opportunity to override the daring of her wild heart.

Once their clothes were back where they belonged–no small feat, given the absurd number of layers that comprised Lenora's attire–he picked up the crate of apples that she'd dropped. "I presume you need to return with this filled, or else run the risk of wagging tongues speculating on what you've been doing alone in the orchard with a notorious rogue for the past hour."

Distress flitted across her countenance. "You're right! This is a disaster. Everyone is going to know what we were doing. I'll be *ruined*, as will my sisters. We'll never be able to show our faces in polite society again, and–"

"And you should take a deep breath." How much more weight could those slender shoulders carry before they broke? He recalled what she'd said before she impulsively kissed him, and his brow creased. No wonder

Lenora was cold as ice. The world as she knew it was burning down around her. If she didn't keep herself frozen, then she'd burn along with it.

Inserting himself into other people's problems was something that he Did Not Do. As a general rule, he absolved himself of all complications, personal or otherwise. A selfish trait that had served him well...until this moment.

He didn't *want* to get involved.

Didn't want to get any more tangled up in her than he already was.

*Walk away,* he told himself. *It doesn't concern you.*

"How many apples do you need?" he heard himself asking.

Oh, for fuck's sake.

"Are you offering to help?" she said, looking as bemused as he felt.

"Let's not make a habit of it."

"A bushel." She closed her eyes and squared her shoulders, silently collecting herself. When her eyes opened again they were calm, almost eerily so, with no hint of the panic that had threatened to overwhelm her mere seconds ago. "A bushel ought to do it. Then Cook will have enough to make pies for dessert. Or maybe we'll have them for dinner, as there won't be time to braise another mutton."

Shoulder to shoulder, they walked through the orchard, accompanied by the quiet hum of busy bees, and the whisper of a breeze stirring through the gnarled branches, and the distant, melodic tolling of a church bell as it rang in the hour.

Seven tolls, Perth counted as he picked an apple. When was the last time he'd been awake to hear such a thing? The life of a bachelor did not lend itself to rising before noon. Sometimes, in the height of the Season when the gambling hells were running at full bore and parties went to all hours of the night, he didn't end his day until the next one was beginning. And never, not once, had it ever occurred to him that he was missing something. That his excessive debauchery was depriving him of anything worthwhile.

But surely this…languidly strolling amidst a grove of trees with the countryside spread out in a green patchwork quilt below him and a pretty girl beside him…surely this was better than waking with his head in a chamber pot, sloshing into the bath to wash off the stench of perfume and ale, then staggering out to do it all over again.

And for what?

For the pursuit of idle amusements?

Or to keep himself constantly distracted from the fact that his life as he was conducting it lacked any meaning? Any substance? Any one worth rising out of bed at a respectable hour *for*?

As another general rule, Perth did not like revelations. Self-discovered or otherwise.

There was no grand meaning to humankind's existence.

No master plan.

A man was born, raised, fucked beautiful women, and then he died. Along the way, if he was lucky, he'd guzzle a few barrels worth of excellent scotch, ride a good horse or two, and have a laugh.

The end.

But as his gaze strayed to Lenora, he was made to question if there wasn't *more*.

More than drinking, and gambling, and fucking.

More than a blur of revolving mistresses who didn't give a damn about him.

More than a life of excess that had not yet accumulated anything worth keeping.

"You are unusually quiet," Lenora remarked, turning to gently place another apple on top of those that they'd already gathered. Her blue eyes rose to his, and a slender brow arched. "No pithy observations or teasing comments?"

"No," he said shortly.

"Oh." The smile that had started to form on her lips faded and fell away. "Your Grace, what I said before, when I was...when I was upset...you need not pay my words any heed. Simple complications are a normal part of any house party, and I should not have laid them at your feet. I apologize."

"Simple complications," he repeated.

"Yes. Simple complications. Nothing out of the ordinary." Her smile returned, pleasant and unassuming and so practiced that it might as well have come from a puppet on a string.

But Perth wasn't fooled.

He had seen behind the icy wall that she'd surrounded herself with, and he knew her better than that. Maybe not her favorite color, or her birthday, or the song that brought tears to her eyes whenever she heard it. But he *knew* her. The real Lenora. Full of uncertainty, and doubt, and fire. Holding everything together not out of some super strength, but rather sheer force of will.

But even the strongest could crack.

Even the tallest walls could come tumbling down.

And who would be there to catch her when she fell?

*I will.*

The unbidden thought physically halted Perth in his tracks. He wanted to take it back. To deny its existence. To pretend those two words hadn't echoed in his head like a gavel struck in an empty chamber. But he could not. Because they were true. And as he'd told Lenora in the upstairs hall, a person could lie to others all they wanted. But they couldn't lie to themselves.

"Your Grace?" she said uncertainly, drawing his attention to the fact that he was standing frozen in place, as rooted to the ground as an apple tree.

"I…" Earlier than any child should have to, Perth had learned to wear his dark wit like a suit of armor and wield his sarcasm as a knight would a sword. It was his only protection against his father's cruel barbs and vicious attacks. Monmouth had liked nothing better than to kick a dog–or a defenseless boy–when he was down. But if the dog showed no reaction to the pain inflicted upon it, or–worse yet–it curled its lip and sneered, then the duke had moved on to easier prey and Perth was left alone to lick his wounds in private.

Somewhere along the way, he'd stopped taking his armor off. It was its own sort of wall. Designed to shield him from both his enemies and his friends. For the only thing that hurt worse than a blow from someone you hated was a punch from someone you loved.

That, too, he'd learned early.

Because even though he had despised his father, there was a piece of him that had always yearned for Monmouth's approval. Despite the bullying, and the beatings, and the bruises, he had wanted his father's love. Until he started telling himself that it didn't matter. He didn't *need* approval. And he didn't need love. Not from his father. Not from anyone.

But when he attempted to lift his sword and fend off whatever these feelings were that Lenora had invoked, he paled when he discovered that his scabbard was empty. He was defenseless, yet again. And he didn't like it now any more than he had then.

"You…what?" Lenora prompted, a faint line embedding itself in the middle of her ebony brows.

"I…" He selected an apple from the crate and tossed it in the air. Caught it with a snap of his wrist. "I was not aware that mutton required lengthy braising."

*Coward*, he thought in disgust.

But if he was one, then so too was she. Two cowards, one in armor and one in ice.

"Yes, it does," she said. "At least twelve hours, if not more."

"There's always Sir Kensington."

Her eyes narrowed. "We are *not* eating Sir Kensington."

"Merely a suggestion." He bit into the apple. Chewed. "Best get these back to the kitchen."

"Yes." She added one more apple to the crate to replace the one he'd taken out, then nodded. "Best we do that."

They were halfway to the manor, its peaked rooftop in clear view, when Perth halted in the middle of the path. "Lenora."

She was several strides ahead, but her head immediately swiveled at the sound of her name. A touch of censure in her tone, she said quietly, "When we return you…you should not address me so informally."

"Back to Lady Lenora and Your Grace then?"

Her clipped smile didn't quite reach her eyes. "Indeed."

In the hallway and the orchard, they had come together with a reckless abandon that he had never experienced before. With his mistresses, the act of fucking in all its varied forms had become almost mindless. An itch to be scratched. A basic animalistic instinct to be fulfilled. But with Lenora–*Lady* Lenora–it was more.

More feeling.

More emotion.

More depth.

Kissing her, touching her, tasting her…it wasn't just fucking.

It was lovemaking.

In the truest form of the word.

And he'd known what would happen if he crossed that line, but he'd done it anyway. Now, if he didn't do what needed to be done, the consequences he had feared would soon follow. For him, and for her. Consequences that wouldn't seem bad at first, until they began to unravel. Until the thread laid tattered on the ground, releasing the anger. The disappointment. The hurt that could be traced as far back as the Monmouth tree had branches.

He would save her from all that, if he could.

A mercy that wasn't going to seem like a mercy.

Not yet.

But in time, she'd see it for what it was. Because he was going to make her see him for who *he* was. For who his father had been. For who he might someday become.

A monster in duke's clothing.

"I cannot marry you," he said flatly.

"Odd, I do not recall proposing."

Having braced himself for tears or outrage or a combination of both, he frowned at her dry response. "I'm serious, Lenora."

"*Lady* Lenora." Her head tilted. "Is this unwarranted proclamation because of what happened in the orchard?"

"Yes, it's because of what happened in the orchard!" How was she so bloody calm? He was tempted to take her by the shoulders and give her a shake. Just enough to rattle all that cool elegance. "And it's not an unwarranted proclamation. Most women of your station would presume an engagement would be forthcoming after finding themselves flat on their back. But I'm here to tell you–"

"That you cannot marry me," she finished for him. "Duly noted."

"You're not…." He broke off, scowling, and switched the apple crate to his other arm.

"Upset? Angry? Devastated that a man who courted my social ruin by kissing me outside of wedlock has declared that he has no intention of marrying me? I'm twenty-four, Your Grace. Far past the age where I collect buttercups and pull off their petals as I sing does my sweetheart love me or does he not. You've made no attempt to disguise your roguish behavior, and as I've said before, your reputation precedes you. I am under no illusion that your intentions towards me were ever honorable."

When the devil had they switched places?

*He* was supposed to be the callous, unfeeling bastard leaving a trail of broken heats in his wake and she…she *was* supposed to be devastated, damnit!

Because that would mean that she cared.

And suddenly he was the one left wanting mercy.

"Good," he bit out. "Glad we cleared that up."

"As am I." She paused. "Was there something else you cared to discuss, or…?"

"No." And he stomped past her to the house to deliver the apples.

AS LENORA WATCHED PERTH walk away, she consoled her aching heart with the knowledge that she'd done the right thing. The necessary thing. The thing that would protect them both.

She could not marry the Duke of Monmouth.

In her head, that much was clear.

But in her tender, hopeful heart…in her heart, there whispered a question.

*Why not?*

To which her answer was devastatingly simple.

Love.

She knew what it felt like to lose the ones that she loved. Her mother. Her father. Her brother. There was no other hurt like it in the world. It was an ache that lingered. A heavy sorrow that never completely dissipated, like a misting autumn rain that went on, and on, and on.

If she let herself, if she gave herself permission…she would fall in love with Perth. She *was* falling in love with him. With his debonair charm and his infuriating arrogance and his kisses.

Oh, his kisses.

But she needed to exercise caution. She needed to remain in control of her sensibilities. Because even as her heart ran recklessly ahead, already dreaming of ivory veils, her head remained firmly mired in the practical.

1) She could not marry Perth because it was widely known that Perth had absolutely no interest in marrying. As proven by their most recent conversation.

2) She could not marry Perth because then no one would remain to look after her sisters or Clarenmore Park.

3) She could not marry Perth because he might break her heart.

Of course, there were no certainties with *anyone*. Not in life or in love. But she had a far better chance of avoiding hurt and heartache with a staid, practical gentleman than an impulsive, seductive rogue. Thus, when Perth had broached the subject (with all the delicacy of an over boiled potato), she'd taken the initiative upon herself to make it clear, in no uncertain terms, that *she* didn't want to marry *him*.

Hurt the one you loved before they could hurt you.

It was the responsible, adult decision.

As for the faint, feeble flutter of longing that had its wings wrapped around her heart…that would fade soon enough. When the house party ended and Perth was out of sight, so too would he be out of mind.

In the meantime, she had far greater things to concern herself with.

"Did Mr. Barnaby and Tom have success with the pipe?" she asked, pulling Mrs. Weidman aside as soon as she entered the house.

The housekeeper nodded with enthusiasm. "They did, my lady. Tom knew just what to do. The water has receded from the kitchen, and Cook only put up a small fuss when I had her move to the summer house." Mrs. Weidman lowered her voice. "Between you and me, I think she prefers it out there away from everyone, but you'll never hear her admit it. The hens were generous with their eggs this morn, and she's already whipped up a dozen soufflés. The smell absolutely divine. The guests are going to love them."

"Are they awake?"

"About half, I'd say. I had the maids set up tables and chairs on the side terrace. I thought eating outside would put some cheer on their faces." Mrs. Weidman gave a conspiratorial wink. "And set the mood for an old-fashioned country breakfast, as you said. Your sisters are up and milling about. Annie's already returned with the bread, and flirted her way into eight pork shoulders at the butcher's besides. His son is sweet on her, and wouldn't that be a fine match?"

Lenora stared at the housekeeper, unsure whether or not she could believe her own ears. "Then…then everything's all right?"

"Aye, my lady," the housekeeper beamed. "Everything's splendid."

And for a while, it was.

…until it wasn't.

# 15

## *Kidnapped*

FOR SEVEN DAYS, Lenora and Perth managed to avoid each other.

An entire week spent stopping in the doorway to scan the room before entering. And altering the seating arrangement at dinner with some made up excuse about wanting to rotate the seats in order to give everyone ample opportunity to talk to someone they might otherwise not. And when faced with a choice between two separate activities, such as a trip into the village or a sailing expedition on a nearby lake, making it a point to pick different ones.

They were doing *such* a good job at pretending the other did not exist that they forgot to account for fate. Or for the fact that Perth, inexplicably, had started to join

Lord Croft on his early morning walks.

Lenora was on her way back from the stables when she saw him. How could she not? The brooding clouds that had been hanging low in the sky since the night before abruptly parted, and a beam of sunlight went directly to him like a moth to flame. He was without a coat or even a necktie, and he'd rolled his sleeves up to his elbows, leaving a decadent amount of golden skin exposed.

Everything about him was golden.

From his hair, carelessly tousled, to the exposed v of his throat, shining with sweat.

He was chuckling at something Lord Croft had said, teeth flashing white amidst all that gold. Then without warning, as if he were a stag scenting a doe on the breeze, his nostrils flared and his head lifted and his eyes went straight to her.

Twenty yards apart they both stood frozen.

Staring.

No, not staring.

*Devouring.*

That was a far better word for the way he was looking at her, and she was looking at him in return. As if they were two people starved, and each was holding a banquet of sweet delights.

He murmured something undecipherable to Lord Croft. Whatever it was caused the viscount to nod and then walk away, leaving Lenora and Perth alone on the limestone path between the house and the stables with only each other and a blanket of fog slowly unfurling across the ground.

Her chest rose and fell as she drew a shallow breath.

And then she was walking to him and he was walking to her, almost running, really, and they might have collided if not for the last second arrival of some much needed common sense.

"Your Grace," she said, curtsying.

"Lady Lenora," he replied with a bow.

So distant, she thought.

So formal.

So hollow.

Which was exactly what she wanted…wasn't it?

"What were you doing at the barn?" he asked, noting the direction of her travel.

"There is a mare ready to foal. I was checking on her. She belonged to my father, and is very dear."

"A tad late for a foaling, isn't it?"

"She did not take in autumn, as the others did. But this winter our stallion, ah, jumped the fence."

Perth's grinned wickedly. "Good on him."

"No. *Not* good on him." She pursed her lips. "Because of his inability to exert self-control, the mare will have her baby in the height of the summer instead of the spring, and that means it won't be weaned with the others, putting it behind."

"It'll catch up. Or it won't." Perth raised his shoulder

in a shrug. "Either way, nature will have her say. As much as you'd like to, you cannot control everything."

"Do you think I don't *know* that?" she snapped, hurling her words at him like a whip. But they struck their intended target, she was the one who winced. "I apologize, Your Grace. I...I should not have spoken so harshly."

"It's all right. You haven't been sleeping."

She brought her fingertips to the corners of her eyes, and the dark smudges she'd covered so painstakingly with powders and creams. "How did you–"

"Because I haven't either. Every time I close my eyes, I dream of you," he said in a voice of smoke and velvet. He brushed his knuckle across the arch of her cheekbone, then gently captured her wrist and brought her hand to his mouth. Even her heart stilled when he kissed the base of her palm. "I burn too hot one moment, then wake shivering the next. You're a fever, Lenora. And you've infected my blood."

She swallowed hard. Then admitted on a breathless whisper, "I've been dreaming about you too."

His eyes gleamed. "Naughty ones, I hope. Tell me, Lady Lenora, do you wake wet and wanting?"

"Your *Grace–*"

"You do," he said when her cheeks betrayed her.

"That is none of your business," she said primly.

"You're dreaming about *me*, aren't you?"

"Yes, but–"

"What are you doing today?" He returned her wrist and slid his hand behind her neck, fingers kneading the taut, tense muscles beneath her heavy chignon. "What plans do you have written on that long list of yours?"

"P-plans?" Perth's massages, she quickly discovered, were second only to his kisses. Like a cat being petted she moaned and craned her head down, all but curling up on his chest as he continued to work the strain from her nape. "After breakfast, a jester is coming to perform in the ballroom."

"He isn't bringing an acrobat with him, per chance, is he?"

"No, why?"

"Just wondering." He changed the angle of his thumb and she nearly melted into a puddle. "What else?"

"Ah…Bridget is performing another recital this afternoon. Then dinner, of course, and if the skies are clear we'll have telescopes set up in the upper balcony for stargazing."

"Then there is nothing too important that we will miss."

"Miss?" Confused, she pulled out of his embrace. "What do you mean?"

"We–you and I–are going into the village today. By ourselves."

"Oh, I couldn't possibly–"

"I am a duke," he said, his infuriating smirk on full display. "You are the daughter of an earl. Which means you have to do what I say."

Her mouth dropped open. "That is *not* what it means. You conceited, insufferable–"

"Have I ever told you how much I like it when you give me such glowing compliments?"

"I cannot just…just *leave*." She crossed her arms. "Someone needs to be here to organize everything."

"Yes, probably," he agreed. "But that someone isn't going to be you."

"Your Grace–"

"Perth."

She gritted her teeth. "*Perth*–"

"I like that, too. When you say my name." He hesitated. "I'm afraid you're *not* going to like this."

"What do you–Perth!" she shrieked when he scooped her up in his arms and tossed her over his shoulder. "Perth, put me down at *once!*"

"Not to worry," he said, patting her on the bottom. "I have it all under control."

FROM THE OPPOSITE CORNER of the sprightly phaeton, Lenora glared icy daggers at him.

"Out with it," Perth said mildly as he expertly guided the horse, a high-stepping gray gelding, around a bend in the road.

Jacobson may not have been able to procure him an axe, but the trusty valet come through with a vehicle on a moment's notice.

Better yet, he hadn't asked any questions.

An admirable trait in a servant.

"You. Have. *Kidnapped.* Me," Lenora said, punctuating each word as she might the end of a sentence.

Perth risked a glance at her out of the corner of his eye. He didn't want to meet her frosty gaze full-on. He'd read the fables as a child. He knew what happened when a man was foolish enough to look at an enraged woman.

And Lenora was spitting mad.

"Kidnapped is a very strong accusation."

Her hand slapped the leather seat. "Then what would you call carrying me against my will to the barn, throwing me into a carriage, and driving me to heaven knows where?"

"A much needed holiday?" he suggested.

"*Ohhhhh.*"

"We're almost there." He slowed the phaeton as they approached a bridge arching over a stream. The gelding's hooves clip-clopped on the wood, the echoing vibrations scaring a school of trout that swam out of their shaded hiding spot in a flash of silver. "See that?" he asked, but Lenora merely set her jaw and turned away from him.

Perth sighed.

All right.

So he *had* kidnapped her.

But what else was he supposed to do? Continue on for the next two weeks in a state of constant misery? He enjoyed the occasional bit of pain with his pleasure in the bedroom, but he wasn't a bloody masochist.

He missed Lenora.

There. He admitted it.

They were living in the same damned house, and he missed her.

He missed her eyes.

He missed her blushes.

He missed her magnificent bosom.

His missed their sparring.

And he missed the taste of her mouth.

God, did he miss that.

During their short ride east of the estate, the sun had finally managed to break through the clouds. It shone brightly, bringing with it all the heat that accompanied a summer in July. Crossing the bridge, he placed the carriage under the sweeping boughs of a willow tree for the comfort of the horse, and then–risking being turned to stone–focused his full attention on Lenora.

"I am sorry I gave you no choice in the matter," he said solemnly. "But if I had asked you to abandon Clarenmore Park and your duties for the entirety of the day to come have a picnic with me, your answer would have been no."

"Yes, it would have been!" she burst out. Then she

blinked. "Did you say picnic?"

Leaning forward, Perth removed the wicker basket he'd shoved beneath the seat and tipped open the lid to reveal a loaf of fresh bread, a jar of jam, cold meats, cubes of cheeses, sliced apples, and peach cobbler left over from last night's dessert.

Lenora peered in the basket, studied its contents, and raised her stunned gaze to his. "How…how did you *do* all this?" she said, gesturing at the food and the phaeton with an incredulous sweep of her arm.

"I am a duke," he said smugly. "It's what we do."

"A duke," she muttered under her breath as he secured the reins and walked around the rear of the carriage to help her step down. "It's what we *do*. Have you ever listened to yourself and how utterly *ridiculous* you sound?"

"Give me your hand," he said, and with a great show of reluctance she extended her arm and he swung her easily to the ground. But when he went to touch her waist she moved deftly to the side, blue eyes sparking with a delightful show of temper.

"We should be staying away from each other," she said, scowling.

"That would probably be best," he acknowledged.

"You don't want to marry."

Watching her carefully, he gave a slight shake of his head.

"I cannot be your mistress."

Another shake.

"Then what are we *doing?*" she cried, flinging her arms out to the side. "Other than risking my reputation? Or have you no care for that?"

"I care," he growled as his own temper rose up to match hers. A single stride, and his hands were on her shoulders, his groin was against her belly, his legs were spread on either side of her dainty feet. "I care too damned much to continue on with this game we've been playing where we ignore each other during the day and dream of each other at night. I may not be able to give you what you deserve, Lenora, but I can damned well give you what you need."

"And what's that?" she demanded, throwing her head back to glare at him.

"*This.*" He kissed her ravenously, and after less than a second's pause she returned his kiss with a fierceness that nearly sent him stumbling.

Passion slammed into him when he sank his teeth into her bottom lip and she released a mewling cry. He soothed the bite with his tongue, then slid inside the soft, moist recess of her mouth to lick and lap and taste.

Seven days.

Seven days since he'd touched her, and it felt like a bloody lifetime.

Never had he experienced a desire like this. To have, to hold, to keep. His heart beat with it. His cock throbbed with it. His entire fucking body shook with it. Shook for *her*. The raven-haired minx he'd kissed on a whim and craved ever since.

He didn't just want her in his bed. That went without saying. He wanted her everywhere. He wanted *everything* about her. Her lips, her breasts, her quim. But also her smile, her laugh, the notch that appeared in her brows whenever he said something that she found particularly exasperating.

She wasn't wearing a crinoline, and when he backed up against the willow tree, his mouth hot against her neck, he was able to bunch her skirts up around her hips with ease. Her tender muscles clenched around his finger when he entered her, to the first knuckle, then the second, and finally the third, her quim already wet and ready to receive him. He circled slowly, then partially withdrew and lightly tapped her clit, teasing the swollen bud until she was panting for release, her thighs trembling against his as she rubbed herself restlessly against the rough bark of the tree.

"This is what you want, isn't it?" he murmured in her ear. "To have me inside of you. Claiming you. Possessing you. Making you come. Take another finger, Lenora. Take it."

She did, and on a groan he unbuttoned his trousers and took himself in hand, fingers encircling the base of his cock as he began to stroke himself in tandem with the two fingers that were sliding in and out of that slippery heat. For all their passionate diversions, they'd not yet reached climax in tandem, and he wanted that connection. For himself, as much as for her.

Thus, when the peak approached, they raced towards it together. Even their breaths linked. And as they teetered on the edge, he ordered her to open her eyes.

"Look at me," he said roughly. "*Look.*"

Thick ebony lashes parted to reveal blue irises glinting with lust. Her pupils were dilated. Her gaze unfocused. It sharpened the instant before she came. Before she wrapped her legs around his arm and cried out. And in that flicker of awareness, in that blissful moment that only existed in the in-between, Perth found his own release.

And it was heavenly.

"I AM STILL MAD AT YOU," Lenora huffed as she helped Perth spread out the horse blanket that he'd nabbed from the stables. It smelled of straw, and there was a patch of dried mud on the corner, but otherwise it made for a fine makeshift quilt upon which they could sit and eat without worrying about ants marching across their legs.

"Here," he said, tearing off a crust of bread and spreading a thick layer of jam across it. "Eat this. An orgasm and food is my recipe for overcoming any bad mood."

When a smile teased the corners of her mouth, she stuffed it with bread. She wasn't about to reward his wicked behavior by laughing. He may have partially redeemed himself, but he'd *still* kidnapped her. Even though she was grateful to be here, in the calm and the quiet, with no problems to solve or seating arrangements to fix or broken pipes to dwell on.

Not that she was about to tell *him* that.

They ate until they were too full to move, and then she put her head on his lap and he idly combed his fingers through her hair while she dozed in the late morning sun. At some point she grew so relaxed and content in his embrace that she fell asleep, and woke to discover the sun had already reached its highest point and was beginning to descend.

"What time is it?" she gasped, sitting upright.

"Does it matter?" Perth stretched and rubbed his eyes, his heavy lids revealing that he, too, had fallen victim to slumber. "We don't have anywhere to be."

"Speak for yourself." There were so many things she needed to do! Had she already missed Bridget's recital? Granted, she'd been present for dozens and dozens over the years. But she did not want her sister to be disappointed. Then Eloise had a fitting scheduled for her ball gown, and if Lenora wasn't there to quite literally hold her in place, she knew that Eloise would miss it. After that was dinner, and what would the other guests think if she was absent? But when she tried to stand up,

Perth grabbed her by the waist and hauled her back against his chest.

"No," he said, nuzzling her neck.

"*No?* I have things to do!" She pushed at the strong arms locked around her body, but it was useless. "Perth, release me this second."

"The world isn't going to come tumbling out of the sky just because you step out of it for an afternoon." He kissed her shoulder. "You're not Atlas. You're permitted to have a life of your own, Lenora. To pursue your own joys away from your sisters and that bloody estate that you wear like a yoke around your neck."

"It could come tumbling down," she muttered even as she slumped against him. "You don't know. And I love Clarenmore Park. It's not as if it's a burden."

Perth snorted.

"Not *much* of a burden, anyway," she amended. "Someone needs to care for it."

"Does that someone have to be you? I've practically written an entire book on how to shirk your responsibilities, if you're interested." He ran his fingertips up her ribcage, tickling her into a giggle. "It's a fascinating read."

She swatted his hand away. "Is being a duke such a grand responsibility, then?"

"Only when I'm made to attend house parties against my will."

"You're free to leave at any time."

"That *was* my plan."

"And now?"

"It's not."

# 16

## *Family is a Burden*

To LENORA'S surprise–and general annoyance–no one even seemed to notice that she'd been missing for the entire day. Not her sisters, or the guests, or even Mrs. Weidman, who greeted her as she entered the foyer with a sunny smile and asked if she'd enjoyed the watercress soup at dinner.

"Yes," she answered automatically. "It was most agreeable."

Perth was right, then, she mused as she made her way through the house. The world *wouldn't* come tumbling down if she left it for a while.

What an extraordinary revelation.

Both outside and in the manor, the hour was growing late. The lights were dim. Perth had gone to his chambers, and nearly everyone else was crowded into the balcony over the west end terrace for a chance to gaze at the stars.

Raising her hand to her mouth and smiling into her curled knuckles, Lenora climbed the stairs with a bounce in her step. She felt as if she had air under her feet, and for the first time since her mother had died, there were butterflies in her heart again.

In all the rush and the turmoil, she'd forgotten what it was like.

To experience genuine *happiness*.

For all his faults–of which, admittedly, there were many–Perth made her happy. He made her smile. He made her remember who she was before she became everything for everyone else.

When she was with him, whether they were bickering or kissing, the rest of the world just…melted away. All of her worries. Her concerns. Her strife.

He took it from her.

He took it, and he cast it into the wind.

Like dandelions seeds on a sweet summer breeze.

And it wasn't forever.

Perth was not the sort of man that a woman spent forever with.

She knew that. Deep down, she knew. But she would take for now. Whether that now lasted a day, a week, or the rest of the house party, she'd selfishly take it. And guard it. And hold it close. Because she'd rather feel like this for a second than endure a lifetime without knowing what it was to love. However fleeting that love turned out to be.

Humming a lilting melody under her breath, one that her nanny had sang to her when she was little, she entered the Crescent Room expecting to find her sisters…and stopped short when, instead, she found herself confronted by Richard.

"What…" Her gaze darted, desperately searching the room for a friendly face, but there was none to be found. It was just her and Richard, whose countenance was decidedly less than cordial. "What are you doing here, cousin? Is there something you need? I can send for a maid–"

"This matter will not be settled by a maid." His flat, glassy eyes took on an eerie glow as he took a step towards her. A trick of the candlelight that lifted the tiny hairs on the nape of Lenora's neck. "Why don't you close the door? We can have a chat. Just family."

"I…" Wrapped up in Perth and her duties as hostess, she'd let her concerns regarding Richard slip by the wayside. He hadn't said anything. Done anything. And thus, foolishly, she had allowed herself to believe that his intentions were not as dishonorable as she'd originally suspected. A mistake, she realized as her throat constricted and an icy chill slithered down her back. A terrible mistake. "I should really go see about a seating issue for tomorrow's breakfast. If you'll excuse me–"

"Close the door, Lenora."

A memory, long pushed aside, resurfaced. Of them as children, playing in the garden while Richard's mother had kept a watchful eye. While Lenora and Annabel had chased each other in circles and Eloise had toddled along trailing her blanket behind her, Richard had sat hunched over in the shade of an Elm tree.

"Come play with us!" Lenora had invited brightly, but their cousin had only shook his head.

"What is he working on?" Annabel had asked, drawing close.

"I'm not sure."

Curious, the two sisters had snuck up behind Richard…and gasped at what they saw.

He'd had a butterfly pinched lightly between his fingers. Its green and gold wings flapped madly as it had attempted to escape, but he'd held firm. Then one by one, he had begun tearing its wings from its body.

"Stop!" Lenora had cried, her stomach queasy at the sight. "You're hurting it!"

"No I'm not," he'd said before he held up the butterfly, now nothing more than a long, wriggling black worm. "It's still alive. It doesn't even need its wings." And he'd tossed it in a jar along with a leaf and sealed the lid.

There had been something wrong about him even then, Lenora thought as she closed the door but remained in front of it with her fingers on the handle. It was more than being different or odd. Bridget, with her nose more in a book than out of it, was different. Eloise, with her penchant for climbing trees, was odd. But they'd never torn apart an insect while it was breathing and stuffed its mangled body behind glass.

Twisted.

That was the word that came to mind.

Something was twisted inside of Richard.

And while she didn't fear he would cause her physical harm, there were other ways to inflict pain.

"What do you want?" she asked warily.

"To have a discussion." He smiled, showing his teeth. "That's all."

"About what?"

"Oh, I have a feeling you know the answer to that."

She did. Of course she did. But she wasn't going to say it until he made her.

"If this in regard to your accommodations, I agree. Your room can be drafty. "I'll–"

"James is dead," he said flatly.

Lenora paled. She'd thought the same herself. Countless times. But to hear it spoken aloud by someone else…it sounded wrong. It *felt* wrong.

"No," she said, vehement in her denial. "We've no proof of that."

"You've no proof that he's alive, either," Richard countered.

"The letter–"

229

"The letter was a forgery. And not even a good one, at that. But it did provide me with the evidence I need to file a case with the Court of Probate, and for that I must thank you."

"You've filed a case?" she said numbly. "For...for what reason?"

His top lip curled in a sneer. "Aren't you supposed to be the smart one?"

"You cannot have Clarenmore Park." She stiffened, bracing herself for battle. The outcome may have been inevitable, but that didn't mean Richard would get there without enduring some pain of his own. She'd not make it easy for him. If he meant to take what rightfully belonged to her and her sisters, then they would fight him every step of the way. It was the least they could do to honor the memories of those they'd loved and lost.

Had their father wanted the estate and title to pass to his nephew, he'd have put it in his will. But there was no will. No reason to have one created, for who'd have ever dreamt that the late Earl of Clarenmore would go walking on the ice that day, or that his heir would go missing soon after? Both gone far before their time. And she'd be damned before she permitted Richard to step into their place.

"That is not your decision to make, cousin. Once the case is filed, the outcome shall be decreed by the presiding judge, Sir Edward Hannen. Are you familiar with His Honor?"

"No," she bit out.

"Ah, that's a shame. Judge Hannen's son and I attended Eton together." Richard leered in triumph. "He is a fair man. I am confident that he'll look out for you and your sisters' best interests, and see that you are given a ward who can ensure you are properly cared for. As your cousin and only male relative, I am pleased to say that I am a perfect fit for the position. As I'm sure Judge Hannah will agree."

Lenora stared at Richard in shock.

*This* was his plan?

It was even worse than she'd imagined.

Losing Clarenmore Park was one thing, but being legally placed in Richard's care…that was something else entirely.

He would have full control over them. Where they resided. Who they married. Even what they wore, if it came down to it.

She knew she could speak for her sisters when she said they'd rather be destitute and living on the street than be forced to obey Richard's every whim. They would be butterflies. Stripped of their wings and forced to live in a tiny glass jar with no way out.

"A judge cannot do that!" Anger chased the fear, pushing her away from the door. Her hands balled into fists. Her eyes flashed not with ice, but with fire. "We are women full grown and thus far too old to be made subject to a ward. You may be able to bend the law, cousin, but even you cannot break it."

Richard made a *tsking* sound and raised his hands, palms out, as if he were addressing a wild animal. "Lenora, Lenora…there is no need to become so upset. I understand that you are prone to fits of hysteria–"

"Fits of hysteria?" she said incredulously.

"–and that has contributed to Clarenmore Park's sad state of affairs, but help is on the horizon. I'd never allow you or your sisters to be locked away in bedlam. Such an awful place, I'm told. Certainly not fit for four bright young ladies with their entire futures ahead of them. With a little guidance and plenty of rest, Dr. Atwood has assured me that you'll make a full recovery. Your sisters as well. Poor dears," he sighed. "How you have suffered. But no more."

"Dr. Atwood?" Her mind raced. What game was Richard playing now? A dangerous one, she surmised. A very dangerous one. "I've never met a doctor by that name."

"It's even worse than I feared." Richard shook his head. "Dr. Atwood warned that this might happen. It's all in the notes he's written. Notes I will have to turn over to the court, you understand. I don't want to," he said with feigned earnestness. "But neither can I stand idly by, nor watch as your manic episodes grow progressively worse. Enough is enough. It's evident that you need watching over before you hurt yourself…or your sisters."

Lenora gasped. "I would *never* do anything to hurt

them!"

"I am afraid that is not what you told Dr. Atwood."

"Lying. You're lying, Richard! And it's despicable." Tears stung the corners of her eyes. Because now she understood. She understood that this had never just been about Clarenmore Park and the house in Grosvenor Square and the title. Richard did not want wealth and property. What he craved most was what his mother had always denied him: control. And through conniving maliciousness, he'd finally found a way to seize it.

Having a woman committed to a mental asylum was appallingly easy. All it took was a husband's word or, in this case, a doctor paid to write whatever Richard told him. Anything she said in her own defense would be disregarded. She'd have no legal avenue to protect herself, or Annabel, or Bridget, or Eloise. For if Richard could do this to her, then there was nothing to stop him from doing the same to them.

She could be a ward of bedlam, or she could agree to be a ward of her cousin, effectively signing away whatever small legal rights she was allotted in order to maintain whatever small freedoms Richard permitted her and her sisters to have.

Her choice was as simple–and odious–as that.

"This is a lot to take in. I can see that." He studied her with his dead fish eyes as if she were a specimen in one of his jars. The faintest hint of a smile, cold and calculating, curved his mouth. "Please know that I only want what is best for you, cousin. With James dead, it falls to me to look after you. It is a job I take most seriously, as I know too that it is what your mother and father would have wanted."

"Get out," she whispered. When he didn't move, she screamed it. *"GET OUT!"*

He bowed, as if they'd reached the end of a pleasant conversation over tea.

She scrambled out of his way when he went to the door, loathe to even breathe the same *air* as him, let alone allow him to touch her. Richard was a monster. A monster hiding in plain sight. And she cursed herself for not checking beneath the bed to see how sharp his fangs had grown.

"There is *one* more thing." He paused in the doorway. "I have long desired a wife, but have been unable to procure one."

"I cannot imagine why," she snapped.

His lips thinned. "Should Eloise be amendable to marriage, I might be persuaded to lose the notes that Dr. Atwood has collected. You would be permitted to remain at Clarenmore Park as a guest instead of a ward, and we might put all of this...unpleasantness...behind us."

Lenora's face went completely blank.

More than twisted.

Broken.

Richard was broken.

"You want to marry your *cousin*?" Disgust coiled in

her like a snake.

"It is not so unusual," Richard defended. "Prince Alfred of Liechtenstein wed his cousin, Princess Henriette. Our own Prince Albert and Queen Victoria were cousins. Some might even say it is a common practice that ensures bloodlines are kept pure."

"I used to feel pity for you. Smaller, weaker, and paler than all the rest of us. Always sitting by yourself while others played. But even animals can sense when something is wrong with one of their own. Were we in the wild, you'd have been left to die long ago." She pointed her finger at him. Threats to herself were one thing, but a threat to her sister? She'd see him dead before he ever laid a single finger on Eloise. "You're disgusting, Richard. And if you honestly think that I would ever, in a thousand years, permit you to marry Eloise, then *you* are the one that belongs in bedlam."

"You'll regret this," he said in a low, ominous tone as splotches of fury married his ghostly white skin.

"The only thing I regret is inviting you here in the first place. A mistake on my part, but one that can be easily rectified. Pack your things and leave. Tonight." At her full height Lenora remained several inches shorter than her cousin, but she still managed to look down her nose at him. "Clarenmore Park is not yours yet, and you are not welcome here any longer."

"You cannot remove me!" he said in the shrill, petulant tone of a child that had just been informed it couldn't have any more sweets. "I'll do worse than send you to an asylum. You'll beg me for mercy on your knees before I'm through with you!"

In her father's study, Lenora had refrained from throwing a book at Perth as it would have been unseemly to physically harm another person, and a duke at that. In the Crescent Room, she had no such ladylike convictions.

The round vase was short but heavy. Lifting it off the table with both hands, she launched it at Richard with all her strength. He yelped and cowered when it struck him squarely on the shoulder, then jumped an inch off in the air when it shattered loudly on the floor.

"That was oddly satisfying," she said, brushing her hands together. "Leave, Richard. *Now*. Or else I'll find something sharper to throw than a vase."

"You're—you're insane!" he cried before he wrested the door open and staggered through it.

"No, I am a Rosewood." Adrenaline coursed through her veins as she followed him to the top of the stairs, determined to ensure that he did, in fact, leave. A temporary solution to a permanent problem, but she knew that she wouldn't be able to sleep until he was gone. "And we protect our own, no matter the cost."

Stumbling, lurching, almost falling, Richard ran down the stairs and disappeared from sight.

In the stillness that followed his departure, Lenora drew a ragged breath. She could *hear* the blood rushing in her ears. Her fingers were numb. Her mind felt clouded, as it sometimes did when she woke from a terrible nightmare.

Dear heavens.

What were they going to do?

What were they going to *do?*

When her entire body began to tremble and then shake, she slid to the ground, buried her head in her hands, and wept.

# 17

## *Consequences*

LENORA DID NOT sleep a wink that night. Tossing and turning, she spent more time staring at the ceiling than the inside of her eyelids. When a new day dawned, she remained in bed, her soul as tired as her body.

Was all this to be for nothing, then?

The sacrifices she'd made. The struggles she'd endured. All in an effort to keep Clarenmore Park afloat. To give her sisters a chance at a new Season. To give her brother time to make it back home.

Now it was going to be snatched away...and what could she do to stop it?

As a female, her powers were woefully limited.

For as much as she had poured her sweat and blood and tears into her family's ancestral home, it wasn't *hers*.

Without a written will, inheritance law bequeathed it to the next male relative. Which was James. But if Richard already had a judge in his pocket, then the estate was already as good as his.

The estate…and she and her sisters along with it.

A brisk knock at the door, and then Bree entered.

"My lady, are you still abed?" The maid went straight to the windows and began to open the curtains, letting a wash of sunlight into the room and causing Lenora to squint. "Lady Donegall was asking for you. She wants to take her daughters on a tour of the stables, and then a ride if we've a placid enough mount. I said that I was sure we did, but I wanted to check with–*my lady*," Bree gasped, having finally turned and gotten her first full look at her mistress. "You…you…"

"If I look as poorly as I feel, then I'm not fit for anyone's eyes. But duty calls, doesn't it?" She smiled humorlessly. "A pitcher of cold water, if you would, Bree. And as much as that eye powder that Annabel swears by as you can muster."

"Is…is there anything else you need, my lady?" Bree asked in a hushed tone.

"The water, the eye powder, and my blue dress with the yellow stripes." She swung her legs over the side of the bed, and gritting her teeth, forced herself to stand upright. "I'll see to the rest."

Thankfully, the lady's maid seemed to intuitively sense that she wasn't up for idle chatter, and after an hour of preening and soaking her face, puffy from shedding so many tears, in cold wash cloths, she was, if not her *most* presentable, at least *tolerably* presentable.

Enough so that Eloise, who passed her in the hallway, did not suspect anything was amiss. Nor did Bridget, who was plunking away at the pianoforte in the parlor for the benefit of a small audience sipping their morning tea. Annabel most likely would have commented on shadows under her eyes that even a heavy layer of powder hadn't been able to completely conceal, but after waiting for Lenora, she'd taken it upon herself to show Lady Donegall and her daughters to the stables.

And that was how Lenora preferred it. That was how she *wanted* it. Not for her sisters to be alarmed, or upset, but for them to enjoy however much ignorant bliss they were allotted for as long as they were allotted it.

If a chicken was to be snatched up by a fox, wouldn't it be kinder that it had no knowledge of its fate until it actually happened? Richard may have had a plan in place, but it would take time to enact it. To get his papers in order, and stain the necessary hands with coin, and coerce whatever other letters he required from Dr. Atwood. In the meantime, her sisters could enjoy the thrill of a normal Season…quite possibly their last.

She wouldn't take that from them.

Not when she had nothing else to give.

After listening to Bridget in the parlor and making herself engage in the small talk that she'd managed to avoid with Bree, she went to the only place she could think of to find some small amount of solace.

Her father's study.

She was standing in front of a sash window, gazing out at his much beloved view of the horse pastures, when the creak of a floorboard revealed that she was no longer alone. Her first thought–her first fear–was that Richard had sought her out to turn the knife even deeper, although she had no reason to believe he remained at Clarenmore Park, as she hadn't yet seen him.

"There you are," said Perth, his deep voice rolling over her like a comforting blanket. "I've been searching everywhere for you. Into the brandy already, are we?"

Already smiling, she pivoted to face him, a jest about the last time they'd been in this room poised and ready on her lips. But when her eyes fell upon his achingly handsome countenance, her throat closed up. And to her bewildered mortification, she once again burst into tears.

"*Lenora.*" He was at her side in an instant, and he didn't collect her into his arms so much as she dove into them. "What is it? What the devil is wrong? Has another pipe burst? Because we'll find a bloody plumber. The best my absurd wealth can buy. Then someone to take a gander at the roof, as God knows the entire thing needs replacing before we find ourselves buried under a mountain of plaster." As he spoke he rubbed her back in wide, soothing circles, allowing her to soak his satin waistcoat with her tears while he continued speaking in a

241

crooning, melodic tune. "The floors could use a sanding as well. And while we're down there, we might as well examine the foundation. Drop a marble in this place and it'll roll from one end to the other."

"You-you-you want to fix Clarenmore Park?" she sniffled.

He gently lifted a damp strand of hair off her cheek and tucked it behind her ear. "I can't have you living in a deathtrap, can I?"

"It doesn't matter." When a fresh torrent of sobs began to build in her chest, she fought them back. "It doesn't matter."

"What doesn't matter, love?"

"Clarenmore Park." Slowly, haltingly, while Perth continued to hold her, she told him everything that Richard had said. When she was finished, when every last, horrible threat had been shared, she lapsed into a silent exhaustion.

And Perth calmly, carefully, said four short words.

"He's a dead man."

"What?" Startled, Lenora followed him to the door when he abruptly set her aside and stalked out of the study and down the hall to the main foyer. "Perth, where are you going? Perth, what are you going to *do?*"

"Stay here, Lenora," he said without turning around.

"But–"

"*Stay here.*"

As he stormed from the house, Bridget joined her in

the foyer.

"What's happened?" she asked, her fair brow creased in concern.

"I…" Lenora placed a hand over her thunderously beating heart. "I'm not certain, but I think the Duke of Monmouth is going to murder Cousin Richard."

THIS TIME, Perth did not bother asking his valet to find him an axe. He did not require a weapon. Richard Rosewood was a cock that he fully intended to throttle with his bare hands.

Lenora said that she'd told her cousin to leave, but weasels rarely abandoned a fresh kill. And that's what Richard was. A fucking weasel who no longer deserved to breathe the same air as the rest of the human race.

He'd had the gall, the sheer *audacity*, to go after the woman that Perth loved.

That he'd do anything to protect.

That had stolen his heart.

Even from their first kiss.

Perth should have recognized the signs. They'd been there all along. Dogging him like a shadow. But how did you describe green to a person who had never seen color? How did you tell them that the life they'd thought was so full was in fact empty? Empty, and waiting. For an impertinent, blue-eyed minx to come along and change everything for the better.

He Was A Person Who Walked Now.

Who'd have ever imagined *that* was possible?

And his drinking had lessened.

Not stopped.

He wasn't, nor would he ever be, a saint.

But he no longer needed whisky to fill those long hours between dusk and dawn. He had Lenora to sustain him. Or at least, the image of her. In the hallway. On his coat. Against a tree. If he had his way, he'd soon have more images to draw from. And Richard, with his lies and his conniving, had dared *threaten* that?

Perth almost felt sorry for the bastard and what was coming his way.

Almost.

"Where?" he snarled at the first footman that he encountered. "Where is the cousin?"

"Mr. R-Rosewood?" the servant replied.

"Yes."

The footman pointed a trembling arm at the stoned courtyard in front of the stables where a man, thin and grossly pale, was climbing up into a town coach.

Perth's lips peeled back in a menacing grin.

He was going to enjoy this.

"ROSEWOOD!" he shouted.

Richard had already seated himself, but he poked his head out the open door, a frown already etched into his bony countenance. "Yes? What is the–Your Grace," he exclaimed, his eyes widening. "To what do I owe this unexpected pleasure?"

When Perth was a child, he had faced down a bully and he had lost.

Repeatedly.

But he wasn't a child any more.

And this time, he was going to protect what he held most dear.

A glare at Richard's livery hand sent the fellow wisely slinking away. After securing the horses to a hitching post, his driver followed suit, and then it was just Perth and his quarry.

He could have given Richard ample warning.

Could have requested that he exit the carriage of his volition.

That's what a gentleman would have done.

But the Duke of Monmouth was no gentleman.

He reached into the town coach and grabbed Richard by the collar of his bright orange tailcoat. Even if Lenora's cousin hadn't schemed to have her thrown in bedlam, his choice in clothing was offensive enough to earn him at least one punch to that smarmy face.

Perth gave him two.

Then another to the nose for good measure.

"What?" Richard cried, reeling forward and cupping his hands over his nose as blood spurted in a satisfying arc of red. "What?"

Shaking out his fist–he'd never seriously punched anyone before, and it bloody well hurt a lot more than he'd been anticipating–Perth made a slow circle around Richard as he used a fancy silk handkerchief to try to stem the bleeding.

It wasn't working.

"I think you broke my nose!" he wailed.

"Hopefully."

"But *why?* What have I done to you?"

"To me?" Perth said. "Nothing. Although now that I'm thinking back on it, you were damned annoying at school. Always sniveling about this and that. Running to the professors to tattle over every little thing."

Richard shook his head in confusion. "But…but that was years ago!"

"Yes, you're right, it was." Like a strike of lightning, Perth seized Richard by the throat and slammed him against the town coach with such force that the massive vehicle swayed from side to side. His face an inch from Richard's, he squeezed his hands tighter and snarled, "But you threatened Lenora and her sisters just last night, you cowardly piece of shite. And I'm afraid that was a mistake."

Richard's eyes rolled in his head. He struck weakly at Perth's arms, trying to dislodge the fingers that were wrapped around his neck in a vicelike grip. His mouth opened and his tongue flopped about like a fish gasping for air, but no sound emerged.

*"Perth! Perth, stop! You're killing him."*

Dimly, he registered the frantic cry of Lenora's voice. It broke through the crimson fog that had descended over his vision, and on a brutal curse he threw Richard to the ground and staggered away from the carriage.

"Are you hurt?" she asked, nearly tripping over her skirts in her haste to get to him.

He caught her before she could fall, and the same hands that had nearly choked the life from her cousin swept up her shaking arms with the utmost care. "No," he said, cupping her face between his palms and stopping a tear with his thumb. "No, I'm not." A tawny brow lifted. "My feelings, maybe, that you thought your spineless rat of a relative had the strength required to do me physical harm."

"Oh, Perth." On a half laugh, half cry, she looped her arms around his back and laid her head on his chest. "While I admire you for your efforts on my behalf, fisticuffs cannot solve this. It's a matter for the courts. There is nothing that you, or I, can do."

"I beg to differ," he said stiffly. "Watch this."

He walked over to where Richard was moaning on the ground and yanked him partially upright by his hair. "My good fellow, we seem to have a disagreement on whether or not you have chosen to leave your lovely cousins alone, make no claim upon Clarenmore Park now or in the future, and burn whatever so-called evidence you've acquired.

"Lady Lenora is of the opinion that you'll still insist on bringing the matter up with your judge friend. *I*, on the other hand, believe you're a man of reasonable intelligence, and as such you are capable of comprehending that if you ever, ever so much as *look* at Lenora or any of her sisters in a manner I deem inappropriate, I shall return and be forced to finish all of this unpleasantness that you made me start. What say you, Mr. Rosewood?"

Richard made a whining, unintelligible noise in the back of his throat.

Perth leaned in close. "Sorry, didn't catch that. All the blood got in the way."

"I-I-I won't bother them again," he wheezed. "I swear it."

"Excellent answer." He released his grip, and Richard slumped to the ground.

"Your Grace," Lenora said, her countenance impassive save for the relief swirling in the depths of her beautiful blue eyes. "Would you care to accompany me to the drawing room? There is something there I'd like to show you."

"Lady Lenora, I would be *most* delighted," he drawled.

Neither of them bothered to look back at Richard as they left the stable courtyard behind. He wasn't worthy of their care or compassion. He was nothing. He was no one. And he was never going to darken Clarenmore's door ever again.

FOR THE NEXT fourteen days, Lenora and Perth struggled to keep their hands off each other. Whereas once they'd gone to great pains to avoid coming within a room's distance, now passion was kindled with a single heated glance.

They sated their hungry desires whenever time and opportunity allowed. On morning walks while the rest of the household slept. During another secret picnic. Stealing off like thieves into the sultry summer night after all sought their beds.

Then there was the parlor incident, where they were very nearly discovered. Thankfully, it was Mrs. Weidman who opened the door to find them in a scandalous embrace, and not a guest or one of Lenora's sisters. She and Perth had been reenacting their first kiss, with her playing the reluctant maiden and he the devilish seducer. The housekeeper, bless her, hadn't spoken a word. She just closed the door as quietly as she'd opened it, and then brought Annie over to stand guard.

On the night of the grand ball, Lenora could have danced in Perth's arms forever. It was a torture to part ways, and the sweet irony of it did not escape her. During their first waltz, she was glad to be rid of him. For their last, she was loathe to let him go.

Until the day came that she'd been silently dreading. The day that they hadn't talked about. The day that was an inevitability, even as they pretended it wasn't.

The final day of the house party.

# 18

### *Endings and Beginnings*

"THIS IS IT, THEN," said Perth on the afternoon that everyone was scheduled to depart.

He was one of the last to leave Clarenmore Park. Lenora had already bade farewell to nearly all the guests, with the exception of Lord Croft, who was staying on for an additional week.

For most of the morning, she and Perth had avoided each other out of an unspoken agreement.

Bluntly put, they did not want to say goodbye.

But the moment could not be put off any longer. His carriage was ready; his mother was already inside.

And it was time for him to go.

"Yes," Lenora acknowledged. "It is."

"Richard won't bother you again."

"No, he won't." And for that, she owed Perth a debt she could never repay. The gratitude she had for him was immense. Overshadowed only by the love that pulsed in every fiber of her being.

She loved Perth.

She was *in love* with Perth.

Impossibly.

Irrationally.

Irrevocably.

And there was nothing to be done about it.

Nothing but to smile and say goodbye.

"I guess we're at that part," he said, giving voice to her thoughts.

"Yes. We are." Her cheeks were dry. Her voice was steady. But her heart felt as if it was about to be wrenched out of her chest. And wasn't this the very pain she'd been hoping to avoid?

Logically, she knew when Perth entered his carriage and it went off down the drive, that she would see him again. Far sooner than she once would have wanted.

It was the end of a chapter.

Not a book.

But then why did this farewell seem so momentous? As if they weren't parting ways for a little while, but forever. And maybe they were. Because even if their paths crossed in London, it wouldn't be the same. *They* wouldn't be the same.

This summer, these past four weeks, everything that had occurred at Clarenmore Park…it wasn't going to be repeated. There was no way to replicate it. No space where they might sneak off into an orchard or steal away into a parlor or have a picnic in the shadow of a willow.

Here, they'd been their true selves. Stripped raw to expose all of their hurts, their vulnerabilities, their most ardent wishes. But out there…out there they were who people wanted them to be. Out there she couldn't be wanton, or wicked. Out there she was a lady, a sister, a daughter of an earl…not a siren who met her lover for midnight trysts in the glow of a full moon.

Perth braced his hands on either side of the carriage door, placed a boot on the metal footrest, and prepared to step in. For a minute, he remained frozen. Then he lowered his leg, turned around, and glared at her. "I don't want to leave, and it's all your fault."

"Me?" she said, taken aback. "What have *I* done?"

She had been exceedingly careful not to ask him to stay. She wanted to. More than anything. But surely the only thing worse than the possibility of rejection was being slapped right in the face with it.

Perth was many things.

Sarcastic, gentle, infuriating, kind.

But he wasn't a husband.

He had told her so himself.

And if he wasn't going to be a husband, and she wasn't going to be a mistress, then she had no right to tell him that she loved him. No right to say that she didn't want their time together to end. No right to admit that despite the turmoil brought on by Richard, this past month had been the happiest of her life.

Because of the man standing in front of her.

Scowling.

"You've climbed inside of my heart." He made a fist and thumped it in the middle of his chest. "And you won't leave. It's damned inconvenient."

"I'm sorry," she said stiffly.

He raked his fingers through his hair, dislodging his hat. It fell to the ground, but neither bent to pick it up. They were too busy staring at each other. Blue eyes melting into brown. Wishing, wanting, dreaming…but not daring to say the words that could change everything for them both.

"I don't even like you." He cupped her jaw, his thumb sliding into the groove at her corner of her mouth. "You're far too proper. You'll be a terrible influence on me with all your rule-following. And you're too stubborn."

"So you've said before," she whispered as a fragile hope took hold. A butterfly, newly emerged from its cocoon. Unfurling its damp wings before it took to the sky for the very first time. All anticipation and breathless wonder as the world opened up around it in a glorious unveiling of possibility.

Perth lifted his other arm and cradled her face between

his large hands. As he gazed at her, his expression softened, his scowl fading way. "We'll probably spend half our days disagreeing over something or other."

"Probably."

"Then there is Sir Kensington to contend with."

"We mustn't forget him," she said solemnly.

"Or your sisters. They're going to cause trouble."

"Buckets of it."

"I don't even like you," he repeated. "But I love you. I love you, Lenora."

She smiled tremulously as the butterfly took flight. "I love you too, Perth."

"Enough to marry a rogue like me? It won't be easy," he warned before she could respond. "The Dukes of Monmouth are notoriously bad husbands. Short-tempered, headstrong, and we drink too much brandy."

"About that–"

"I'll give you my heart, but not my Glenavon Scotch," he said with a pained expression. "A scoundrel needs his vices, Lenora, or else word will get out that I've reformed. Do you want people to be under the impression that I have redeeming qualities? Think of my reputation. Please."

The laugh was halfway up her throat before she managed to catch it. "All right," she said with feigned soberness as she slid her hands under the lapels of his frockcoat. "You can keep your vices, such as they are, so long as no harm befalls Sir Kensington."

"If a rooster meets an axe in the middle of the woods and there's no one there to hear him–"

"Then the scoundrel yielding the axe will return to discover his entire liquor cabinet empty.

"You wouldn't," he said, horrified. "Even the scotch?"

"*Especially* the scotch."

"You're a ruthless woman, minx."

"Don't you forget it." Her smile slipped a notch. "I cannot abandon my sisters, Perth. Or Clarenmore Park. We'll travel to London for the Season, but after that I'd like to return here. Not forever. Just until they've found husbands of their own."

"We can use my manor in Grosvenor Square," he said matter-of-factly. "There's more bedrooms, and an oak tree in the rear garden that Eloise should find suitable for all of her climbing endeavors. As for Clarenmore Park, we've already spent half the summer here. What's another year or three? My country estate has an entire staff that can keep it running. To be honest, they'll most likely be glad to be rid of me."

When tears stung, she blinked them away. "You'd do that? Take in three sisters and a drafty old estate?"

He frowned. "I'd do anything for you, Lenora. Absolutely anything. While I cannot promise the road will always be a smooth one, I *can* promise that I'll be loyal. I'll be true. And each night, even if we're annoyed with each other, which will most likely be more nights than we like, I'll kiss you. Just like this." Lowering his head, he brushed his mouth across hers with infinite care. "And you'll know, that even when I'm being too prideful to say the words, that I love you. That you are my heart. That I shall treasure you from the end of this day to the beginning of the next, all the years of our lives."

What could she say to that? Other than...

"Yes." Rising up on her toes, she flung her arms around his neck as warmth enveloped her body. "Yes, I'll marry you. Yes, I'll love you. Yes, I'll always kiss you goodnight. Yes, yes, *yes*."

They kissed after that. For so long, and so ardently, that the carriage driver flicked the reins and drove off, leaving Lenora and Perth in the middle of the drive by themselves, too enthralled with each other to notice. Nor did they notice the three noses pushed against the windowpane.

"Move over," Annabel demanded, jabbing Eloise with her elbow. "I can't see."

"I can't see either," said Bridget.

"They're *still* kissing." Her interest waning, Eloise hopped back from the window and threw herself into the closest chair. "I guess this means they're going to get married."

"A duke for a brother-in-law," Annabel said with a great deal of satisfaction. "Excellent."

"It's terribly romantic," Bridget sniffled.

Eloise looked at her sister aghast. "Are you *crying?*"

"You're not?" Turning from the window, Bridget

plucked an embroidered handkerchief from the silk reticule looped around her wrist and blew loudly into it. "Lenora is in love. Just like in one of my books, except it has happened in real life and it's even better than a fairytale."

"Love. Kissing. Marriage." Eloise wrinkled her nose. "I'd rather eat worms."

"You'll be eating your words when it happens to you," Annabel said pointedly. "Just wait. That will be you out in the drive soon enough."

"Ew. How can they even breathe with their faces all mashed together like that?" Eloise wondered. "When Lenora faints from lack of oxygen, *I'm* not going out there to pick her up."

"Shhh!" Bridget said. "Here they come."

Collectively, the three sisters held their breath as they heard the front door open. A few muffled words were exchanged, and then Lenora and Perth appeared in the drawing room doorway arm in arm.

"We've wonderful news to share," Lenora said, blue eyes sparkling above rosy cheeks. "We–"

"Are getting married," Eloise interrupted. "We saw everything."

"Eloise," Bridget scolded. "You're supposed to let *them* announce the news."

"We're very happy for you," Annabel said. "When is the wedding?"

"We haven't decided on a date yet," said Lenora after

a startled glance at Perth.

He put an arm around her waist. "October."

"So soon?" Bridget's lips parted in dismay. "But that hardly gives us any time to plan!"

"And it is right before the Season starts," Annabel pointed out.

"Next month, then," said the duke. "Is there any food set out? I'm famished."

"Would you excuse us?" Lenora asked her sisters. "I'd like a word with my betrothed."

"Her betrothed." Bridget fanned a hand in front of her face as her eyes brimmed with more tears. "How terribly–"

"If you say romantic again, I'm going to punch you." Exasperated, Eloise grabbed her by the hand. "Come on. Let's give them the privacy they need so that they can kiss some more."

Lenora blushed. "That's not what we're going to do."

"Speak for yourself," Perth said mildly.

She waited until her sisters had quit the room and closed the door behind them to say, "We cannot be married in October. Maybe in the spring–"

"No."

"Why not? There's no reason to rush."

"I know of at least two very good reasons," he countered. "First, I have no intention of giving you time to talk yourself out of marrying England's most renowned and handsome rake."

"Did you just give yourself that title?" she asked suspiciously. "I'm not sure if you can do that."

"Second," he went on, ignoring her, "I want you in my bed. Tonight. With those long, gorgeous legs wrapped around my arse and that tight little quim welcoming my–"

"*Perth!*" she hissed as her blush intensified. "We cannot share a bed. We're not married yet."

He crossed his arms, his mahogany gaze piercing in its intensity. "Exactly."

Heat flared in her belly. Goodness, but when he stared at her like that...when he stared at her like that, was it any wonder that she'd fallen in love with him? He was not who she'd ever envisioned herself marrying. With the exception of being a duke, he was the most *un*suitable groom in existence. Because he was right. They *were* going to argue. And he was too sarcastic by far, just as she tended towards being too serious. Their personalities would be in constant conflict.

But somehow, miraculously, it worked.

*They* worked.

Together.

A rainbow didn't come from clear skies.

And true love didn't always come from perfect harmony.

Sometimes it was born of two souls searching for what they were missing in themselves...and finding it in another.

"I've heard September is a lovely time of year for a wedding," she said, then squealed when Perth swept her off her feet and carried her to the nearest sofa. The air left her lungs as she bounced harmlessly onto the cushions. Sucking in a deep breath, she placed her hand in the middle of his chest as a token measure of resistance when he began to kiss his way down her neck.

"We can't," she said weakly even as she raised her arms above her head and arched her back.

"Why not?" he murmured, teeth tugging at the edge of her bodice.

"Because…" Except for once, she didn't have a good reason. Propriety, etiquette, manners. They were all well and fine. But they weren't what was most important. Love, desire, laughter. *Those* were the things that mattered. Those were the things that sustained a person's soul. "Perth?"

"Hmmm?"

"This time, lock the door."

# EPILOGUE

### *Old Friends*

FROM INSIDE THE carriage that her son had chosen not to get into, the Dowager Duchess of Monmouth folded her hands across her knees and smiled at the empty seat across from her. Filled not with a friend, but with the memory of a dear familiar face.

"We did it, Catherine," she said, even though (truth be told) she'd not really had anything to do with it at all.

The eldest Rosewood daughter wasn't who Anastasia had paired her son with initially, but it was apparent to anyone who looked at them that they were made for each other. Lenora's steadiness would temper Perth's impulsiveness, and when she tended towards coldness he would bring her warmth.

Now they had a wedding to plan! And a nursery to fill.

Not right away, of course. It was important that a husband and wife get to know each other as a couple before they welcomed a sweet babe into their family. But she'd prefer to hold a grandchild in her arms sooner rather than later.

Three, Anastasia decided.

Three would be perfect.

A boy and two girls.

Children who would grow up not in fear of their father, but in love with him. Children who would have their silliest wishes fulfilled, and their dreams granted. Children who would have their curiosity encouraged, and a hand to steady them when they stumbled, and strong arms to carry them to bed when they fell asleep reading on their mother's lap.

Because the Monmouth curse, if ever there was such a thing, was broken.

Perth had not chosen his bride out of obligation, or duty, or a surge of lust that would fade before the ink had dried on the wedding register. He loved Lenora deeply. A mother knew these things, and it was both a privilege and a joy for Anastasia to witness that love, that dedication, and that partnership firsthand.

"I wish you could be here beside me, Catherine," she said softly. "But I feel you in spirit. You're looking down on your girls, and I will make sure to look after them. We've found Lenora her happily-ever-after. Now we shall do the same for Bridget, Annabel, and Eloise…"

# ABOUT THE AUTHOR

Jillian Eaton grew up on a farm in Maine and now lives on a farm in Pennsylvania with her husband, their three children, and a lot of animals! When she isn't writing, Jillian enjoys reading, hiking with her family, and gardening.

She really, really hates laundry.

Printed in Great Britain
by Amazon

85937374R00154